Praise for *Something in the Sea*

'A brilliantly creepy and worryingly enthralling debut' *Daily Mirror*

'An astonishing and gripping story' *Guardian*

'I was gripped and enthralled' William Boyd

'The plot is tight and exciting, and the writing has great authority . . . it gives a sort of "Conrad" feel . . . admirable stuff . . . I was so gripped by the story that there was no way I was going to stop . . . the framing device is absolutely wonderful . . . simultaneously original and traditional . . . I enjoyed reading it enormously' Sara Maitland, Winner of the Somerset Maugham Award, Scottish Writer of the Year

'Difficult to put down . . . the ending is as surprising as it is shocking' *Yorkshire Gazette & Herald*

'Something of an ancient mariner saga . . . curiously hypnotic' *Literary Review*

'A chilling psychological thriller by a debut writer of whom we will certainly hear more' *Daily Mail*

'It kept me turning the pages . . . The description of the storm, for example, is terrific . . . I like the premise too. I like the use of the Little Mermaid fairytale and I think that the device of the story within a story is very effective . . . I enjoyed it a lot'
Patrick Neate, Whitbread Novel Award Winner

SOMETHING IN THE SEA

YVES BONAVERO

BLOOMSBURY

First published 2006
This paperback edition published 2007

Copyright © 2006 by Yves Bonavero

The moral right of the author
has been asserted

Bloomsbury Publishing Plc,
36 Soho Square,
London WID 3QY

A CIP catalogue record for this book
is available from the British Library

ISBN-9780747585862

10 9 8 7 6 5 4 3 2

Typset by Hewer Text UK Ltd, Edinburgh
Printed and bound by Clays Ltd, St Ives plc

Extract from *The Little Mermaid* by Hans Christian Andersen,
copyright © Frederick Warne and Co, 1980

All papers used by Bloomsbury Publishing are natural,
recyclable products made from wood grown in well-managed
forests. The manufacturing processes conform to the
environmental regulations of the country of origin.

www.bloomsbury.com/yvesbonavero

For Anne

I have strange power of speech;
That moment that his face I see,
I know the man that must hear me:
To him my tale I teach.

S.T. Coleridge,
'The Rime of the Ancient Mariner'

I

Beep-beep! beep-beep!
Beep-beep! beep-beep!

That's all it took: eight short shrill beeps.

Game over.

Life over.

Just like that. No warning. Well . . . hardly any.

Yet, up to that day, my life had been plain sailing. An easy cruise on autopilot. A doddle.

Bloody hard work – yes.

But a lot of fun.

Those of my friends who think I'm a smug bastard will tell you I had been incredibly, undeservedly lucky on all counts. You won't have to believe them: perhaps, like me, you think that people make their own luck.

Then all my navigation errors caught up with me.

It is only when attempting to make a landfall, of course, that you find out how accurate your navigation has been. Simple: either you end up in the right place, or you don't. More often than not you find out the hard way: think of all those Armada captains who believed they were steering a safe course back to Spain in the middle of the Atlantic – only to hit the rocks on the west coast of Ireland. Was it their fault if, in their day, nobody knew about the existence of the Gulf Stream?

Mind you, if truth be told (not my forte: I'm a criminal lawyer), I've been off course by more than a couple of degrees over the last few years. Here's an interesting fact: if your heading is erroneous by a mere one degree over a distance of sixty nautical miles, then your cross-track error, as we call it, will amount to one nautical mile. Result: instead of finding the entrance to some snug harbour, you're on the rocks. I, of all people, should have known.

Was it my fault if, on that scorching day, we left the fuel berth in Brindisi too late to make Dubrovnik before nightfall? We had decided to avoid Bari, since it seemed to be totally under the control of the Albanian Mafia. Both our nautical pilot books, everybody we talked to in the ports and marinas we'd called into, from Palermo to Portosirena, from Messina to Roccella Ionica and Crotone, all the tourist guides we carried on board agreed on the wisdom of staying as far away as possible from the Albanians. Now, when Sicilians warn me about crime, I, as a fellow professional, am not inclined to second-guess them.

It is well known that the Mediterranean is rarely ideal for sailing: either it blows a hooligan, or there isn't a whiff of wind. Since we'd left Portosirena, the rather tired marina on the northern coast of Sicily, right opposite the Aeolian Islands, the strongest wind we had encountered had been a pretty useless anticyclonic breeze. Even the much-feared Golfo di Squillace had proved to be a total misnomer, as, in flat calm conditions, we wearily trundled under power across its forty-mile expanse, mainly concerned that Lucy should drink enough to avoid dehydration. If you are not to get confused, I need to clarify one thing straight away: Lucy is our beloved five-year-old angel of a daughter – sorry, I keep forgetting she's six now, we celebrated her birthday last week – and *Miss Lucy* is my pride and joy, our 42-foot Bowman sailing yacht. If you ask me, Bowman yachts are, or rather were, the finest craft built in the UK, which probably explains why the Bowman yard recently had to file for bankruptcy. It's not the quality of your product that counts, it's your marketing skill. That's the world we live in. Never mind: precisely two years, six months and fourteen days ago, thanks to my contacts and expertise, we were lucky enough to acquire the last Bowman 42 from the liquidators, thus fulfilling a lifelong dream. *My* lifelong dream anyway.

How prettily she sits on the water, her low, sleek shape enhanced by the blue line running from bow to stern on her white topside! Gracile, agile, spirited but obedient, lively yet forgiving, a mount fit for a Viking prince. She indulges my foibles, tolerates my whims, balks at no challenge. We are a team, almost a single organism, the nautical equivalent of a Centaur, albeit hopefully less monstrous: half man and half mermaid, perhaps. I trust

3

Miss Lucy with my life, in the knowledge that no other vessel could provide such an exhilarating ride in complete safety. Easy to control too: all the halyards and sheets run back to the cockpit, so that, in theory at least, it is possible to operate her single-handed. Cathy sometimes complains that I spend more time with *Miss Lucy* than with her; it isn't true, but the temptation certainly is there.

Having spent last summer cruising around the Aeolian Islands, we were now on our way to Croatia and its magical, unspoilt 1,185 islands. Just the three of us: Cathy, Lucy and me.

Convincing Cathy to sail to Croatia hadn't been easy. Some years ago, her elder sister, Miranda, was spending a few days in Split with Croatian friends when she suddenly fell ill – some kind of food poisoning. Her condition deteriorated so quickly that her hosts decided to rush her to hospital for what should have been an intensive three-day course of intravenous antibiotics. Unfortunately, the junior doctor on duty injected her with the wrong drug; if I remember correctly, some kind of product designed to stimulate the heart. Miranda then found herself inflating at an alarming rate. On the second and third days, wracked by excruciating abdominal pains, she had complained to the hospital doctor, who rudely reminded her that he had better things to do than listen to the whining of a spoilt western woman. On the fourth day her small intestine burst; she was dying. Her friends snatched her, unconscious, out of the unsupervised splendour of Krizine hospital, and delivered her

4

post-haste, all sirens howling, into shambolic Firule hospital. There, a newly qualified houseman decided she was too young to die. With minutes to spare, he put her guts together; then, assisted by a posse of devoted nurses, off duty as well as on duty, he looked after her day and night for weeks on end. Two months later, Miranda had got rid of her infection, lost four stone and recovered intestinal continuity. Cathy had been doubly traumatised by her sister's experience: shocked that Miranda should have been at death's door, and appalled by the medical negligence that had nearly killed her. The result has been to instil deep prejudice in Cathy, who fundamentally wants no truck with a country that, according to her, has nearly killed her sister.

Nevertheless, armed with glossy pictures of idyllic secluded islands, unpolluted warm waters and permanently blue skies, after months of patient advocacy, I had prevailed. Cathy had eventually accepted that, in the unlikely event of health problems developing on board, her own medical competence was more than sufficient to protect us from the vagaries of the locals. At last, we were on our way.

In spite of their sensible use of sun creams, my two women were turning a richer hue of gold every day. They did not mind the absence of wind; in fact, they were naturally happier motoring through this enervating heat wave than they would have been holding on for dear life in the sort of force six sirocco I kept praying for. Anyway, the weather was pleasant enough for a family cruise, and Cathy and I alternated at the wheel, keeping our watches short – two hours – in order to fight the boredom that, added to the heat and the low drone of the engine, could easily lead to sleepiness.

All this motoring meant that we needed to refuel before crossing the Adriatic. Having eliminated Bari, our only bunkering option was Brindisi, which we had reached in the early evening. Again, Brindisi isn't the kind of city that gets rave reviews in the Lonely Planet guide, but, arriving from the sea, it was majestic enough. We berthed alongside the low stone quay opposite the town, right at the foot of the monumental staircase built by Mussolini to highlight the end of the Via Appia. There were no facilities, no water, electricity or toilets, but the mooring was secure and the well-tended garden that surrounded the monument was quiet without being spooky. After dinner, I took a waterbus across to the city, to check the location and opening hours of the fuel berth. It was manned (after a fashion) by Pietro, a semi-retired ruffian whom my patient investigations traced, within less than an hour, to the counter of a dark, smoke-filled establishment nowhere near the sea front. I found out that the pump would be open at seven the following morning, bought Pietro a beer and thanked him for the information with the most effusive gesticulations I could conjure up; finally, pointing alternately at my yacht across the harbour and at the phosphorescent hands of my diving watch, I imparted to him that *Miss Lucy* would be moored in front of his pump at a quarter to seven. The fact that I speak only five words of Italian was no serious hindrance, since none of the sounds emitted by

Pietro seemed to belong to any Latin language. We solemnly shook hands, and I returned to *Miss Lucy* with the relief and quiet satisfaction that follow a successful reconnaissance mission. Although the crossing from Brindisi to Dubrovnik, at nearly one hundred miles, is significantly longer than from Bari, I was hoping that, in the middle of summer, it should be possible to do most, if not all of it, during daylight hours – which, ideally, meant leaving at first light.

As I got back on board, Lucy was already asleep. She wore only a small pair of knickers and a sleeveless T-shirt; yet, as I softly kissed it, her forehead was moist with perspiration. She smelt of baby oil, sun and salted caramel.

'Is she asleep?' Cathy whispered as I entered the forecabin, where she was lying naked on the V-berth.

'Like an angel,' I confirmed.

Cathy smiled and put her book down. She likes detective stories, maybe because she never guesses who the murderer is; I gave them up when I went to law school.

I folded up my shorts and T-shirt and lowered myself on to the bunk between her long, suntanned legs.

At dawn, Cathy insisted on getting up to help me move the boat across, so that we were already moored at the fuel berth by six-thirty. The bustle of the previous night had been replaced by an eerie quiet. Lucy was still deep asleep in her bunk, her breathing sweet and regular. She had woken up once, but a glass of water and a hug had been enough to send her back to sleep. The only sign of life emanated from a strange street-cleaning contraption, purring in the distance as it slid alongside the waterfront. Cathy went back to bed while I sat in the cockpit, a mug of coffee in hand, putting the final touches to my passage plan. When Pietro finally appeared, eight o'clock had chimed at a nearby belfry, and the temperature was rising rapidly. I waved my hands in histrionic despair, pointing at my watch. Yet the worst news was still to come. Overnight, Pietro had remembered that the level of diesel oil in his tank was very low, so that any attempt to pump it out would likely suck in unhealthy doses of sludge. Not to worry: a road tanker was on its way, and should arrive any minute now.

Nine o'clock.

Ten o'clock.

I was pondering two questions. First, should I leave with an empty fuel tank, and rely on my sails? Unfortunately, the weather forecast did not point to any useful breeze and, becalmed under the July sun for days on end, we might just get very hot and bored. Second, how could one expel Italy, or, at the very least, Brindisi, from the European Union?

We waited. And waited.

By the time we left with a full tank, we had no chance whatsoever of making our landfall before dark. Since I am a fully qualified yacht master, this did not worry me unduly; I am used to night navigation. In fact I like the unique sensation that comes from slicing through the darkest of nights with nil visibility, the boat rocking back and forth to the soothing rhythm of an invisible swell. However, it meant that we would have to rely on Croatian lights, whose dependability was unknown, and also that Cathy, who has no training in night navigation, would be unable to take the helm after dark. After a long and tiring day, we'd probably arrive in a poorly lit port, when all mooring manoeuvres would be difficult. None of this however presented us with an insurmountable challenge, and no sooner were we out on the open seas than I started to relax. We headed almost due north as I set the autopilot on our course for Dubrovnik and sat back to enjoy what promised to be a wonderful day. All around us, the sea was vibrantly blue and lasciviously oily, shimmering as it evaporated under the pitiless Adriatic sun. Due to the high moisture level in the air, the visibility was moderate, perhaps a couple of miles, but not restricted enough to worry me. Cathy brought me a glass of cold apple juice in the cockpit and returned down below to give Lucy her breakfast.

If you know anything about the sea, you will already have noticed how extraordinarily lucky I am. Very few women like the sea. Out of all my sailing mates, not one – *not one* – has a wife or girlfriend who likes sailing. In fact, most hate it. One of my mates says that women are as allergic to the briny as mermaids to dry land: he may have a point. Before we met, Cathy was into walking and mountaineering; her ideal holiday involves trekking in Nepal or Bhutan at a minimum altitude of 10,000 feet above sea level. Maximum? There is no maximum altitude. The higher the better. I, for my part, do not like being higher than Mean Low Water Spring Tides level; in other words, I already get giddy at high tide, let alone in the Himalayas. People with such opposite tastes are normally incompatible. Not Cathy and I, though: my wife has taken to sailing like a duck to water. She even trained to Competent Crew level, which means just that: competent. When I tell my friends that she's the most competent doctor I've ever met, they shake their heads and smile – but it's true. She sailed through her medical studies, started work as a GP seven years ago, aged twenty-seven, and is by far the most popular doctor in her practice. Not only does she get diagnosis and treatment mostly right, but I think her patients sense that she really cares. And she managed to produce our little blue-eyed Lucy, who is now five. Sorry – six. Why is she growing up so fast?

Forgive me if I appear to repeat myself – but this is how lucky I am. With Cathy, I have on board a wife, a cook, a doctor, a first mate – and a lover. I mustn't downplay the lover. For, in the course of our annual cruising fortnight, we seem to make love more often than during the remaining fifty weeks of the year. You know how it is. The pressure of busy lives, conflicting schedules, different priorities, permanent stress. The life of a successful modern couple. Slightly out of control? Possibly.

The last few months have been more hectic than usual. Allenby & Brook, my firm, combines criminal law and family law; as a result, we were inundated with new clients following Operation Ore. You may recall Operation Ore: it was mounted by the UK police on a national basis after they received from their American colleagues a list of some six or seven thousand UK citizens who had paid by credit card to view pictures of naked children on the Internet. America loves policing the world; additional piquancy in this case stemmed from the fact that, out of the 250 new child-porn sites that crop up every year, more than half originate in the States. Dozens of family men from all walks of life – doctors, workers, police chiefs, teachers, salesmen, judges even – streamed to our offices in search of legal advice. In addition to criminal proceedings, many of them quickly became embroiled in messy separations or divorces, which were then handled by Sarah, our family-law partner, and her expanding team. I couldn't help feeling sorry for a couple of these fellows, who were being hounded, their reputations shattered, their families destroyed, for what might have been a momentary lapse of judgement. What misfortune caused them to be titillated by pictures of minors? What compulsion led them to risk everything? I guess those are questions for psychiatrists. As lawyers, we were doing well: Allenby & Brook's fee income doubled in six months, with my department leading the charge. Everybody in my team was working sixteen to eighteen hours a day. Except for a few hours' sleep, I had hardly been home for weeks, and was utterly exhausted. More often than not, when I finally made it home, Cathy would be out on call or working nights. Whenever our paths crossed, we argued: she felt I was spending far too much time in the office, and doubted that my clients were worth defending. Reminding her that they were innocent until proved guilty failed to impress her. Thankfully the firm had just recruited a couple of juniors to help with the backlog, but for the time being they were just additional hassle. Furthermore, your average fifty-year-old dentist is unlikely to want to discuss his pornographic web-surfing habits in front of some lass just out of law school. In fact the pressure had kept increasing right till my departure, by which time I had practically reached breaking point. For some reason, Operation Ore was getting to me. In my recurring nightmares, wide-eyed kids were silently sobbing on the Court benches while I masterfully orchestrated the legal defence of their abusers. I had to get away. Cast off. Put as much clear blue water as possible between that office and me. Mind you, even on the boat, I had to turn off my mobile phone on day one in order to stop the stream of increasingly frantic voice and text messages from the office.

Christ, how impatiently I had been waiting for this sailing holiday! I was desperate to get away from the slime of Operation Ore and be reunited with my wife and daughter. Indeed, after so many weeks spent practically without seeing Cathy, I sometimes wondered whether husband and wife shouldn't make it a rule to work together, as the persistent lure of illicit sex in the office or the surgery might contribute more than domestic routine ever will to a healthy relationship.

Anyway, there we were, husband, wife and daughter. All three of us afloat at last. Which reminds me of yet another of Cathy's functions aboard *Miss Lucy*: Lucy's mum. Pretty crucial, since small children on boats demand full-time attention. Yes, I am lucky with that woman. I am not quite sure about her precise surgical qualifications, but, should an emergency arise, would trust her entirely to perform an appendectomy on board. The amount of drugs, medicines, medical and surgical equipment we carry on *Miss Lucy* is phenomenal, and far exceeds our stock of victuals. Sometimes I wonder whether I am sailing a yacht or a floating hospital; indeed, there are no bacteria we could not vanquish, few viruses we could not keep at bay, hardly any wounds or traumas we could not sterilise, stitch up and dress. And then there are the eye-drops, the ear-drops, the insect-bite creams, the rehydration powders, the bandages and gauzes, the painkillers and sleeping pills, the stethoscope and blood-pressure monitor . . . our two biggest lockers are crammed full with Cathy's medical junk. I don't really object, since I know that she would be reluctant to embark on prolonged cruises in foreign waters – let alone to Croatia – without the comfort of this mobile surgery. She has a point, of course: young children at sea are constantly at risk, however closely one tries to supervise them. The biggest risk, however, is falling overboard and drowning. I suspect that, in such an emergency, my first-aid skills might prove as valuable as all of Cathy's stuff, but, frankly, I prefer to avoid dwelling on nightmare scenarios.

This isn't always possible, of course; nor would it be advisable, since a keen awareness of dangers remains the mariner's best insurance policy. For example, I was in two minds when, early that afternoon, Lucy asked to go swimming. We were not halfway yet, and I did not want to waste too much time. On the other hand, the temperature had risen well above thirty degrees Celsius, and, in the total absence of wind, only the slight breeze produced by the boat's steady motion provided any relief. Unfortunately, the fierceness of the sun made it impossible to sojourn on the foredeck, where the motion-induced airstream was best enjoyed; Cathy and Lucy soon had to retreat to the cockpit, where we all sheltered in the sweltering shade of the blue sun awning.

It's funny how some people, even excellent swimmers, are afraid to swim in the open sea. Somehow, the idea of the abyss underneath, the hundreds of yards, miles even, of unfathomable marine life right underneath their soft underbelly and dangling parts spooks them, as though they were expecting attacks from the deep at any moment. It probably comes from watching Hollywood movies, too many of which, like *Jaws*, have infected the collective unconscious. Cathy tends to be apprehensive of the invisible mysteries and alien inhabitants of the deep. My own views are more prosaic: I hold that the waters are less likely to be polluted offshore than near the coasts, and that, in the open sea, there are no currents, rollers or breaking waves to jeopardise swimmers – and yet . . . in all honesty, I must confess to feeling a certain frisson whenever we lower the sails or stop the engine in order to swim *in the middle of the sea*. I suppose that, deep down, we all associate the idea of swimming with that of shallow waters next to safe shores and friendly beaches – dry refuges to which, as noisy toddlers, we used to run when attacked by marine monsters.

'Terence, please, look at Lucy,' Cathy said.

I did not like what I saw. My baby was red-faced and puffed-up, like a child with a high fever.

'I can't keep her cool,' Cathy continued. 'I've tried everything, from wet towels to cold drinks. It's just too hot.'

I made an instant decision.

'Fine,' I said. 'I could do with a break myself. Let's stop now, have a swim, cool down and have a bite. All right?'

No sooner had the engine stopped than we realised how loud it had been. Not that my Volvo engine, with its underwater exhaust, is particularly noisy; but the reason I sail is to get away from machinery. The silence was now blissfully restful, yet so perfect as to be almost oppressive. We revelled in it, drifting slowly at the centre of our own happy, circular, self-contained universe. Even the VHF radio had stopped crackling. For a while, we observed how the brutal assault of the vertical sunrays was repelled by the water's minute undulations, which playfully, almost mockingly, reflected light and heat back to outer space, turning the surface into a dazzling mirror. Strange, how the sea manages to keep its privacy inviolate and yield none of its mysteries even in extreme sunlight. This made me realise that the object of my own fears wasn't some possible creature of the deep, but the opposite. I wasn't, never had been, afraid of something in the sea. But what if there was nothing under that shimmering surface? Now, that is a spooky thought. Just imagine: what if the immeasurable depths under my keel are in fact a bottomless void, a trapdoor to hell – worse, a shortcut to oblivion?

'Well?' I asked Lucy. 'Are you ready to jump in?'

Without taking her thumb out of her mouth, she nodded with a beguiling smile.

'Wait a minute,' Cathy interjected. 'She hasn't got her armbands on.'

While Cathy kitted our daughter out, I lowered the ladder from the swimming platform into the water. In reality, Lucy could more or less swim by herself, but neither Cathy nor I were keen to discard her rubber rings. I stayed on board while my two beautiful girls swam in slow circles around *Miss Lucy*, keeping a watchful eye on them as well as scanning the horizon in case any shipping suddenly pricked the circumference of our hazy bubble. I secured the lifebuoy to a mooring cleat on the port quarter and sat down next to it, ready to throw the ring should Cathy develop a cramp – which she was prone to – or show any sign of distress.

I dipped in after Cathy and Lucy had climbed back on board, taking the opportunity to check the stern gear and the engine raw-water inlet in case we'd picked up any ropes or debris. Cathy often wonders what sort of debris one could possibly pick up in the clean, unpolluted waters of the open sea. She seems to forget that these open waters are Italian, which, I am sorry to say, means that they contain a fair amount of plastic bags, bottles, old fishing nets, polypropylene ropes and other indestructible flotsam that can easily block your raw-water inlets or foul your propeller.

By the time I got back on board, Cathy had knocked together a salade niçoise – lettuce, tomatoes, eggs she'd boiled the previous evening, anchovies and locally grown capers we'd bought in Lipari, all in a generous dose of peppery olive oil – and some dry Sicilian goats' cheese. Refreshed by her swim, Lucy ate well and nearly fell asleep before we could carry her below decks for her afternoon nap. I plotted our position on the Admiralty chart, entered the time in the logbook and restarted the engine. Soon we'd resumed our northward voyage, at a speed of some seven or eight knots. When Lucy woke up after a couple of hours – the combination of heat, engine drone and the boat's slow rocking motion always had a soporific effect on her – I went down below to play with her and read her a story. Cathy stayed at the helm for several hours while we went through Hans Christian Andersen's *Little Mermaid* from beginning to end, after which, in order to console Lucy, I installed her in front of paper and crayons, so that she could copy the book's illustrations. Well, perhaps I am overstating the case slightly, since one might easily have missed the likeness between original and copy. A slight frown on her adorable face, stealing occasional shy glances at me, Lucy looked older than her years as she concentrated on the job for the best part of an hour, while I nodded off. Not once did she ask the dreaded question: 'Daddy, are we nearly there?' For a while, I also tried to keep vaguely attuned to the crackling of our VHF set relaying Channel 16, the international emergency frequency. It is a sad fact that, in Mediterranean waters, numerous idiots seem compelled to encumber Channel 16 with whistling noises, dog barks, music or obscene talk. Others tend to use it as a ship-to-ship chatting frequency, in complete contravention of the rules. It is tempting, when this happens, to turn the volume down, which I eventually did.

I relieved Cathy as, exactly on our port beam, undaunted by the haze, the sun was putting up a last display of volcanic orange and sanguinolent red. Wondrous as it was, after this furnace of a day, I was glad to watch it eventually sink under the sea, until the pale halo to the west had merged with the omnipresent electrical activity that kept zigzagging across the skies in quick flashes.

We were still a couple of hours out of Dubrovnik when I knew we were going to be hit by a thunderstorm. Although we were well within the theoretical range of the main Dubrovnik approach light, there was no glimpse of it, due to the combination of poor visibility and sheet lightning. These Mediterranean storms can hit you from nowhere and with no warning, generating phenomenal gusts in their midst. Soon the sky was ablaze. Curiously, there was no thunder. Nor, initially, was there any wind. It felt like watching a silent film. The proverbial lull before the storm? I sent Cathy and Lucy down below, on a mission to close all portholes, batten down the hatches and stow away loose items. I also told them to put on their automatic life jackets since, storm or no storm, it is good practice to wear them at night.

'Mummy, are we going to be sick?' Lucy asked in a small voice.

Cathy looked at me.

'I don't think so, my pet,' I answered. 'We're not far from Dubrovnik. We'll be there before you know it.'

'Come on, darling,' Cathy called. 'Let's get you into your Little Mermaid pyjamas, and then you can wear your nice red life jacket on top.'

As they disappeared down the companionway hatch, I was still idly wondering whether to rig a tiny forestaysail or some kind of storm jib in case something really nasty turned up. Given the feeble breeze that was just rising, it seemed somewhat ridiculous, yet I felt uneasy. Anyway, before I could finish my deliberations, it was on us. An invisible fist smacked me so hard that I nearly fell backwards. It came from the west, so fast that the boat was already heeling thirty degrees to starboard before I could react. Within minutes our red ensign and Croatian courtesy flag had been shredded to pieces and blown away by the squall that was howling through the rigging like a demented soul. I swung the wheel hard to port in order to turn *Miss Lucy* to windward, facing the gale. She immediately righted herself, but started vibrating like a machine-gun under the pounding assault of the short, sharp chop that quickly built up. Being a seaworthy, solidly built yacht, even under bare poles my Bowman felt stable and easy to steer to windward, although I had dropped our speed to somewhere around two knots. In the knowledge that this would be no more than a short-lived squall, I felt quite exhilarated by the show, only worried that the girls might get seasick and a bit panicky in the confined saloon. However, there was no way for me to leave the helm at this juncture, as the autopilot's reaction time was far too long to ensure that the boat's bow was kept facing the wind. The chop was getting steeper and more brutal all the time, but I knew that, in an average storm, it would take hours for the seas to reach their full force; by then we'd be safely moored in Dubrovnik.

After an hour or so, I had to admit that this did not feel like an average blow. The sky was incandescent, glowing with flashes of lightning so close together in space and time that the whole seascape was lit by a funereal half-light. All the ropes and pulleys, the stays, shrouds and halyards frantically flapped about in a cacophony of high-pitched shrieks and whistles. The urge to go down and reassure the girls was overpowering, but I still couldn't risk leaving the helm. Hoping that Cathy might open the hatch and get within shouting distance, I had to continue driving straight into this maelstrom, although we were now turning our back on Dubrovnik. I hoped to God this would indeed turn out to be a short-lived, localised storm, since, on this westerly heading, we'd end up back in the middle of the Adriatic. I reassured myself that the barometer, when I'd last checked it, had been quite stable and that no gale warning had been broadcast on VHF, until I remembered turning the volume down so low that I might easily have missed one. Should I turn around and flee before this gale? I did not doubt *Miss Lucy*'s ability to outrun it, but knew that, should it go on for any length of time, we'd soon get dangerously close to the numerous outlying rocks and islands along the Croatian coast. The wind strength was still increasing, and the worst gusts must have exceeded sixty or seventy knots. The wind-driven spray sounded and felt like shrapnel as it hit the cockpit cover and my face. Water started streaming in. Some of it was solid green water shipped over the bows when some eight- or nine-foot wave started breaking before the boat had a chance to rise, some was accumulated spray, glowing pink through the lightning. Another half hour elapsed; I was getting tired, but the boat was still handling the worsening conditions fairly comfortably. The seas weren't that high, but short and ferocious. Time and again, *Miss Lucy* would rise up and briefly hesitate at the top of a steep wall before skidding down again, and I was proud of her. I never had a chance to get my oilies or boots out and was soaked to the bones but, more than from the cold, I was shivering from the sheer excitement of it all. In fact neither air nor water were cold. As far as I could tell in the prevailing din, there was still no thunder, although the electrical frenzy all around us had turned night into day.

The strange luminosity reminded me of an unnerving experience I had the summer Lucy was born. I was on watch on a friend's ketch, on my own, in the middle of the Indian Ocean, on a quiet and starry night. There was no moon. Suddenly, without the slightest warning, the sea had instantly turned into a riotous, luminescent, boiling cauldron. I had never seen anything like it. My initial wonder gave way to panic as, without the slightest breeze, the absolute stillness had been supplanted by loud splashing noises, and pitch darkness by clouds of incandescent spray. The racket! It had taken me a while to think of an explanation. As far as the eye could see, great phalanxes of gleaming dolphins, dozens, scores, untold legions of them, were wildly prancing about, their greenish, phosphorescent underbelly stripes turning water into bright seething lava. Dolphins! Even after I had identified the phenomenon, I remained scared: they were powerful, almost mythical beings, and their behaviour was weird. Then, just before daybreak, as though by magic, they all simultaneously dived. Disappeared. At the end of that watch, as the stillest of dawns lazily painted the orient pink, I was still shaking; yet I had subsequently failed to convince my sceptical crew of the veracity of my account.

But this Adriatic squall was no windless dolphins' visitation; far from it. The waves were getting nastier by the minute, though they still remained of moderate height, if only because the wind kept blowing the top off them. I found the shelter of the spray hood more and more indispensable to protect my eyes from the salt water that was hurled at my face at supersonic speed. As I hunched down at the wheel, I lost forward visibility, which made the task of negotiating each breaking wave much more difficult. Some of the bigger seas caught me by surprise, pounding the hull and foredeck like sledge-hammers. Ceaselessly assaulted by their white foaming tops, *Miss Lucy* began to show signs of stress. And still I did not know how the girls were faring down below.

Just as I was beginning to wonder whether, perhaps, the wind had stopped freshening, a gargantuan roar put me right. The sun awning, complete with straps, Velcro fastenings and stainless-steel tubes, was ripped off, lifted and instantly dismantled. Not only did it tear up the canvas of the spray hood, but it also remained caught in various places, so that I was surrounded by metal tubing and all manner of straps and canvas strips all wildly flapping about, damaging the deck and hull wherever they happened to make contact, all threatening to knock me down. Blinded by the spray pellets, knee-deep in the water now freely accumulating in the supposedly self-draining cockpit, I had no option but to let go of the wheel to try and subdue the crazed monster. It was lashing out in all directions, flailing about at such speed that it was impossible for the naked eye to perceive the flying bits. I started frantically slashing all the straps and fastenings that I could reach with my pocket knife. But my faithful knife couldn't protect me from the one-inch-thick metal tube that whizzed past my ear before crashing on my left elbow. I nearly passed out with pain. The boat, broadside to the seas, was now rolling like a drunken pig. She was heavily heeling to leeward, reeling under the constant assault on her rigging, lacking time to right herself between one breaking wave and another.

Cathy immediately knew that something had happened. Every other word was drowned by the wind as, popping her head through the companionway hatch, she shouted at the top of her voice: 'Terence! Terence, are . . . OK? For God's sake, what . . .?'

The rest of her question was swept overboard.

My mouth was so dry that I found it difficult to articulate.

'No problem!' I yelled back. 'The fucking cover has been blown away. That's all. We'll be OK!'

'Do you want . . . radio for help?' she screamed.

'No! Don't worry! The worst is behind us!'

'What? What . . . behind us?'

'HOLD ON!' I shouted – too late.

A huge bastard of a roaring wave nearly capsized *Miss Lucy* as it crashed on our port side, drenching both of us under tons of water. Cathy hit her head hard against the frame of the hatch as dozens, maybe hundreds of gallons cascaded down the companionway through the opening. How I managed to stay on board with only one good hand I'll never know.

Just then Lucy's shriek reached our ears, obliterating everything else for several seconds. Cathy darted straight back down below, closing the hatch behind her. I grabbed the wheel with my right hand and, applying full power with my knee, brought the yacht's nose back up into the wind, where she stabilised a little. I knew that trying to lash the wheel in position would be a waste of time, so tried to steer with my foot while frantically slashing all remaining ropes and straps to get rid of the goddamned sun awning. All of a sudden, much to my astonishment, the tangled mess of canvas, straps and metal took off vertically. We were dealing with some kind of *trombo marine* – that much was clear. One of those tornadoes that occur in the Med, much less infrequently than you would think. Lady Luck still wasn't smiling on us: the crosstree, the radar bracket and the radar reflector caught large amounts of the ascending bits and pieces. One after the other, I heard stainless-steel bolts snap. One after the other, like murderous hail-stones, I heard five or six of these heavy projectiles crash all around me. I couldn't see them, but felt a couple whistling past my ears before burying themselves in the cockpit sole, inches from my toes. All the while I was anxiously looking up and trying to guess where the radar was most likely to fall – not that I could have got out of the way to save my life – so that several vicious seas caught me by surprise, pounding the boat with devastating force. I tried to analyse the situation calmly, but the most coherent thought I could summon was 'Shit! Shit! Shit!' followed, in quick but orderly succession, by 'Shit! Shit! Shit!' It worked. The last remnants of the cockpit cover, reduced to ragged tentacles, suddenly let go of my boat and flew straight to hell. Held by the last couple of bolts, but looking precariously wonky, the radar stayed up.

At this moment, I knew that my affair with Sarah was over. And that I wouldn't miss her.

Do not misunderstand me.

First, I am no superstitious Sicilian fishwife. In this instant realisation, there was nothing akin to a deal with God. No life-changing vow. No plea bargain. None of the usual save-me-now-and-I-promise-to-behave-later stuff. In fact, I don't think I was really fearing for our lives. Not consciously anyway.

Second, of course I shall miss her. I shall miss Sarah

greatly. I shall miss her softly closing my office door, prim and proper in officious black skirt and pinstriped jacket, and then sitting on my desk, legs crossed high enough to reveal the absence of knickers. I shall miss her incisive wit, her wicked sense of humour, the swelling of her dark nipples and above all the modesty of her demands. I shall miss her laughter and her sharp tongue, her inquisitive fingers and her legal acumen. Her mocking admiration. Her easy availability. Just as my prospects of making it to partner were ripening, I probably would have to change firms, in order to avoid bumping into her twice a day. Life without her would lose its edge, much of its brilliance and most of its fragrance.

And yet I wouldn't miss her, because my life was complete without her. And at least it would continue. Which is what I want more than anything. All I want is to see Lucy grow up. To grow old with Cathy.

They say that, when faced with imminent and brutal death, you see your whole life flash before your eyes. I always found this hard to comprehend. What I can now say, however, is that all of these thoughts flooded my mind instantaneously. I knew *instanter*, to use legal jargon, that the woman of my life was in the same boat as me, clinging to our daughter, and trusting me to negotiate this storm. Trusting me with her life and that of our child.

I forced myself to calm down and took stock of the situation. My left arm was inoperative; the elbow was swelling by the minute, and the excruciating initial pain had been replaced by a dull, white ache. In order to reduce the throbbing pain caused by its jerking about, I needed Cathy to put it into a sling as soon as possible. On the positive side, at least the engine was still working perfectly, and I had plenty of fuel. I knew I should have rigged up a fully reefed main and a storm jib in order to provide some stability; it would have been more comfortable than heading straight into the wind under power, and also would have provided me with some insurance against engine breakdown. On the other hand, this squall was so cyclonic that perhaps sails wouldn't have been much help. Heaving-to wasn't possible since, apart from my messed-up rigging and a damaged crosstree, I was in no condition to hoist any sail and did not want to take Cathy away from Lucy. That left the same old two options: continuing as we were, or turning around and running before the storm, maybe trailing warps to slow us down and prevent broaching, until we reached the shelter of the Croatian coast. But how was I supposed to organise these warps with only one hand, and drive the boat at the same time? On reflection, given that this coast was strewn with unlit rocks and unknown to me, simply drifting towards it seemed inordinately risky. Nothing for it, therefore, but to continue motoring at a thirty-degree angle to the wind at the lowest speed compatible with maintaining steerage way; should the engine develop any trouble, we would have to call for help. I could only hope that Cathy was somehow managing below decks.

Deep down, I was seething with anger. It was not directed at the storm, or at the morons who'd failed to forecast it. No, it was directed at the asshole who'd been stupid enough to risk the lives of his beloved wife and daughter. What for? I kept asking myself. *What the bloody hell for?* What right do you have to drown people whose only crime is to love and trust you? Fucking ego trip, if you ask me, all this skipper business. Keep calm. We're going to make it. Nobody is going to get drowned. Not this time. Isn't the wind beginning to subside?

Initially at least, it might have been wishful thinking – but soon I formed the impression that the roaring and frothing were decreasing. After a while, most seas, nasty though they remained, stopped breaking. Within a quarter of an hour the gale had turned into a fresh breeze that was lifting only a moderate amount of spray from the top of the waves. I didn't feel relief yet – just exhaustion, ravenous hunger and nausea at the same time. My arm was aching as though loose, sharp fragments of bones were tearing at muscles and ligaments. It wasn't long before I dared putting the autopilot on and rushed down below.

I had a gut-wrenching feeling of apprehension as I opened the companionway hatch. Yet I was shocked, first by the stench, then by the carnage. Due to the combination of engine heat and lack of ventilation, the inside temperature was at least ten degrees Celsius higher than outside, and the air smelt of bruised apples, warm engine oil and rotten eggs. In the half-light that emanated from a single, twelve-volt wall-lamp, it was clear that the saloon looked different, but at first I couldn't focus on any detail. There was stuff everywhere

– all of it sodden. The water that had come in when Cathy had opened the hatch had filled the saloon; all seats, bunks, sleeping bags were soaked. Most of the contents of the galley lockers were strewn all over the place. Cooking pans and half-melted loaves of bread, limp spaghetti and mobile telephones, crushed tomatoes and wet passports, instant soup sachets and broken lamps, green and yellow peppers, dirty tablecloths, books and pulped magazines – a slimy, chaotic mess. I narrowly avoided a half-empty bottle of Sicilian Extra Virgin olive oil whose contents, right under the last step of the companionway, had emulsified with the seawater, turning the floor into a skating rink. Its label had floated off, and the lurid virgin on it seemed to have acquired a sardonic grin as well as green scaly legs. I was at once concerned and relieved to hear our submersible bilge pump running underneath the saloon sole – it must have been working overtime for the last couple of hours, if only to deal with all the vomit whose traces were sloshing about everywhere. All of this I took in within a couple of seconds, before realising that the soaking blanket lying on the sofa was moving.

'Is that it? . . . Terry – is it over?' Cathy asked in a small voice.

Cathy rarely calls me Terry – an abbreviation neither of us particularly likes. At any rate, I always hated it. I went down the last two steps and attempted to walk over to her, nearly losing my balance as the boat lurched to port.

'Yes.'

My throat was dry, my voice raucous.

'Yes,' I repeated. 'At least I think that's it. I'm sorry. Where is Lucy?'

As Cathy carefully lifted the blanket, out of the half-light Lucy's immobile torso slowly appeared. She seemed fast asleep, almost comatose, her head resting against Cathy's left breast, her arms limp. I couldn't detect any sign of her breathing. It took me a couple of seconds to realise my baby's head was wrapped in one of those tea-towels decorated with silly marine motifs, compass points or weather-forecast areas, that I keep buying on impulse at boat shows. Now the motifs were almost invisible. For some reason, I was reminded of Rembrandt – or do I mean Goya? Anyway, gory battle scenes and mutilations kept flashing before me. *Mother and Child. Descent from the Cross. The Anatomy Lesson* – you name it. The boat kept lurching about violently as the autopilot, too slow to react when thrown off-course by the impact of a bulky sea, then grossly over-compensated, only to be caught off-guard by the next one. Since I depended on my only good arm to hold on to the ceiling grab rail, I couldn't rub my eyes to get rid of this . . . hallucination, so I blinked several times. Closed my eyes. Re-opened them. And again. The towel was still drenched in blood. Sticky with thick black blood. I stared at it uncomprehendingly, my throat too constricted to ask the obvious question.

'She'll be all right,' Cathy whispered.

'What happened?'

'I'm not quite sure. I think she was trying to crawl

towards me when I was talking to you, and then was hurled across the saloon when we got thumped.'

'What . . . what's the matter with her?' I managed to ask.

'She's got some cuts on the head. They always bleed a lot.'

'Will they require stitches?'

'Yes. But obviously I can't do it now. Terence, how are you? What's wrong with your arm?'

'Some stupid metal tube crashed on my elbow.'

'Is it bad?'

'I think it's fucked.'

'Jesus! Are you in pain? Do you want me to come on deck?'

'I'll be fine. You look after Lucy. Did she pass out?'

'I don't think so – or else only for a few seconds. But she's been vomiting the whole time. She's totally drained – as you can see.'

For a couple of seconds, I stood watching my be-draggled little girl, wishing I could touch her. Clearly the fact that Lucy had not lost consciousness for any length of time was good news but, watching her unna-tural immobility and empty stare, I suddenly felt sick.

'Cathy – what do you think?' I asked.

'I think she'll be all right,' she repeated. 'Anyway, there's nothing we can do right now. Terence, you must drink some water – and take some painkillers. You know where they are.'

She was right. I was beginning to dehydrate, and the pain was unbearable. Unfortunately, our drinking-water supplies had been in plastic bottles, all of which had exploded, and our usual painkillers had disappeared together with the galley tray that used to house them. I did not feel inclined to go forward and rummage through Cathy's tons of medical kit – that would have taken for ever, and I needed to go back to the helm. I drank two glasses of stale water from the tap and brought one to Cathy. She gave it back to me after one gulp.

'I don't want to be sick again,' she said, nodding towards Lucy. 'Better wait a while.'

I bent down, pushed the wet hair away from her high forehead, on which the traces of her encounter with the companionway hatch were only too visible, and kissed it.

'You keep resting,' I said. 'We'll be in Dubrovnik in no time.'

She managed a feeble smile.

'Have I heard this before?' she asked. 'I say, skipper, would you kindly try and improve the accuracy of your navigation, please?'

I dropped another quick peck on her forehead, checked our position and heading to destination on the GPS – which miraculously still worked, although it had been thoroughly doused – grabbed my oilskin tops and rushed back to the cockpit.

Around midnight I spotted the Dubrovnik lights. Much as I had suspected, they made no obvious sense. First, the flashing light on the islet of Daksa appeared before the more powerful approach light on Hridi Grebeni; second, neither of them was visible until we got to within three or four miles, although their theoretical range is ten nautical miles. At sea, identifying lights is both vital and exceedingly tricky. Many a mariner has paid the price for having seen what he expected to see, as opposed to what was really there. When attempting to identify any kind of landmark or light, it is essential to keep an open mind, to check and double-check, and to be prepared for surprises.

During the last hour the wind had abated; had we been in the Caribbean, we would have expected another pummelling after crossing the eye of the storm, but this was the Adriatic, and the oppressive calm that had prevailed during the day simply re-established itself. The waves soon disappeared, leaving a heavy swell that in no way hindered our progress. Cathy not only managed to put Lucy in our bunk in the forward cabin without waking her up but, by the time we entered the port of Gruž, she had treated my elbow, first with an ice pack, then with some kind of anti-inflammatory unguent, and put my left arm in a sling. She had also tidied up the saloon to a remarkable extent. Apart from our injuries, the most obvious reminders of our recent ordeal were the ubiquitous slime, the revolting smell and the pile of sodden paper and linen half hidden behind the gimballed cooker in the galley.

Gruž is a commercial port, busy with ships, ferries and cruise liners, devoid of any charm, where arriving yachts are squeezed between a dirty road and a noisy ferry berth. The harbourmaster, the police and the customs are to be found in a large building on the ferry quay, opposite a concrete block from the Communist era called the Hotel Petka. It is compulsory for all boats to clear customs in Gruž, the official port of entry for Dubrovnik, before going on to the peaceful marina a few miles further up at the end of a beautiful inlet resembling a Norwegian fjord. Although my initial plan had not involved spending the night in Gruž, by the time we were safely moored, flying the regulation yellow flag requesting customs, it was one o'clock, and there was no question of leaving in a hurry. In fact, we were quite impressed by the efficiency of the harbourmaster, who found us a space near the end of the quay, whereas, from seaward, no gap was visible between the dozens of tightly packed yachts. Since I was in no position to offer much help, Cathy picked up the mooring line in the semi-darkness all by herself and dealt with it most efficiently. Soon we had secured it as well as two stern lines and our gangplank. I shut the engine down and went below decks to switch off our running lights and re-organise the electrics. Cathy followed me.

'Well, it seems we made it after all,' she said.

'We did. What are we going to do about Lucy?'

Cathy wearily sat down on the settee and reflected for a while.

'I'm not quite sure. Basically, we have two options: Croatian hospital or on-board monitoring. Ideally, we need to get her skull X-rayed as soon as possible.'

'Why? Do you think she might have fractured it?'

She hesitated for a couple of seconds before answering.

'No. Routine precaution. You never know.'

'Did you manage to examine her on the way?'

'Yes – of course. But it's not clear-cut.'

'Why not?'

'Do you really want to know?'

'Of course I do!' I replied impatiently. Cathy is always reluctant to blind me with medical science, a policy that I normally approve of – but there was little normality in our predicament.

'All right,' she answered. 'Good news first: she hasn't lost consciousness. And she is not showing signs of lower cranial nerve palsy. She had no fit or seizure. And I haven't detected any cerebrospinal fluid leak, or bleeding from the ears or nose. However, I cannot be entirely sure about that – as you have seen, she's covered in blood from her cuts.'

'Is she in pain?'

'Right now, she seems to be sleeping reasonably peacefully. I cannot give her any systemic analgesia, or it will be impossible to measure her consciousness and other key neurological signs.'

'OK, doctor – what's the bad news?'

'Well, she's pretty exhausted – almost dazed. She has difficulty concentrating, even keeping her eyes open. She couldn't tell me what happened to her, which suggests amnesia.'

'Amnesia?' I blurted. 'Surely that would be quite serious?'

'Depends how long it lasts. Also, it is hard to assess in infants and young children. They don't pay attention to things the way we do. The other worry is that she's

35

vomited a lot. If it was due to the head injury, it would be very bad news indeed. Could be a sign of raised intra-cranial pressure, which is the key risk. However, it is more likely to have been the result of seasickness.'

I was beginning to understand what she meant when she said it wasn't black and white. Contrary to received opinion, when it comes to delivering clear-cut, useful opinions, doctors are a thousand times worse than lawyers. Find this hard to believe? Just you wait till you get cancer and need to re-draft your will.

'Won't she get better if we let her sleep?' I asked.

'Not necessarily. I wouldn't want her to slide into too deep a slumber. And she needs to drink.'

'What about her cuts?' I asked, trying to sound com-posed. 'Can't you do something about those?'

'Terence, I'm exhausted, and it's the middle of the night. And her cuts are probably the least of her pro-blems. Besides, I'd never choose to operate on Lucy myself if somebody else could do it. You know that.'

Cathy's voice had become a tiny bit shriller. I sat down next to her and took her hand, hoping she wouldn't notice that my own good hand had turned clammy with cold sweat. For a few seconds, the silence between us was pregnant with the taboo prospect of Croatian hospitals. Perhaps it was time to make a decision.

'Of course I know that, darling. I certainly could never do it myself. But taking her to hospital won't be easy. First, we have cleared neither customs nor immigration, which means we'll probably end up in jail as soon as we set foot on Croatian territory. People here tend to be quite bureaucratic, as you know. Second . . .'

'I don't give a damn about bureaucracy,' she interjected. 'You're the lawyer. You bloody well sort the bureaucrats out.'

'OK, my love – I'll take care of the bureaucrats. The question is: is Lucy going to be better off if we charge across Dubrovnik in the middle of the night, or should we all get some rest and get help in the morning?'

'Your guess is as good as mine.'

'What do you mean?'

'I mean that, if we end up spending five hours in a stifling waiting room before seeing some badly trained, harassed junior doctor – that won't do Lucy much good. On the other hand, if she does have a cracked skull, we need to know without delay.'

'What would happen then?'

'She would be monitored very closely.'

'Monitored for what?'

'As I said: monitored for raised pressure inside her skull or brain.'

'What would happen if the pressure went up?'

'You don't want to know.'

Visions of East European plumbers drilling boreholes through Lucy's skull made me dizzy. I looked at Cathy. Her eyes were closed. I cleared my throat.

'Cathy – do you think Lucy has a fractured skull?' My voice was still hoarse.

She reflected for a long time before opening her eyes.

'No – I don't think so. The cuts are obviously superficial, and I couldn't see any signs of major trauma around them. There doesn't seem to be any penetrating head injury. Of course, you often don't see any sign of fractured skull externally if secondary to blunt trauma.' She looked around the saloon. 'However, whatever she fell on is likely to have been made of wood and rounded. On the other hand, the force of the impact would have been crucial – and we know nothing about that. There is also a risk of injury to the spine in the neck region, though Lucy's neck doesn't seem tender. Bottom line: we won't know for sure before we get the X-ray result. Even better, perform a CT scan.'

'Will they have CT scan machines in Croatia?' I asked. Cathy shrugged her shoulders.

'All right,' I went on. 'Suppose we find a hospital. What would happen then?'

'As I just said, Lucy would be closely monitored for complications, such as swelling, bruising or bleeding which can happen inside the skull – or even inside the brain.'

'What kind of monitoring would that be?'

'Regular checks, including shining lights into her eyes, checking her pulse, reflexes, blood pressure, conscious- ness level and so on. She'd be woken and checked throughout the night, perhaps every hour or so.'

'OK,' I said. 'Here is my proposal. Feel free to turn it down. You are the chief medical officer on board this ship, and you know I have blind faith in you. Fact one: it's the middle of the night. Fact two: we're in Dubrovnik; medical facilities unknown but unlikely to be first-rate. Fact three: we have not cleared customs or immigration, and our passports have just disintegrated in hot vinaigrette. Fact five: Lucy seems to be quietly asleep, and most unlikely to be suffering from a cracked skull. Fact five: we're both utterly exhausted. Conclusion: we all get some rest, clear customs and get Lucy's head and my elbow X-rayed first thing in the morning.'

Cathy appeared lost in her thoughts.

'Well?' I asked.

'You've given me two facts five and no fact four,' she said casually.

'I apologise, your honour. Does this mean that the whole of my evidence is inadmissible?'

'No,' she said. 'In fact I'd much rather monitor Lucy myself than rely on the locals. Of course we'll have to check on her regularly.'

'No problem. I'll set my watch to ring every hour. Will this be all right?'

She hesitated.

'I guess so.'

I put my good arm round her shoulders.

'OK, then, doctor. Anyway, if Lucy deteriorates, we can change our plans at any time. By the way, you've been a truly exceptional first mate. Sorry it's been such a nightmare of a day.'

'This at least wasn't under your control, Terence.'

Her choice of words surprised me, but she was looking at the floor.

'I know. Thank you. I'm sorry all the same. The main thing is: we'll be all right. Lucy will be all right. Don't worry. You know how resilient kids are.'

'How is your arm feeling?'

'Not too good. I could use some serious painkillers – I mean, none of this paracetamol stuff for kids.'

'I'll get them for you. Shall we have a quick bite or go straight to bed?'

'First things first: I need a cold beer. Then anything handy. No time for cordon-bleu cuisine.'

'Well, I could use something hot and sticky. What about a bowl of rice?'

'Stupendous.'

I opened two cans of beer while Cathy rummaged in the food lockers.

'Sorry,' she said. 'Afraid the rice is rather soaked in sea water.'

'Does it matter?'

'I guess not. I'll cook it without salt.'

A while later, thanks to the combination of beer and a double dose of manly painkillers – was it a double dose of beer as well? – I was beginning to feel much better. In spite of the still-oppressive heat, the warm rice was working wonders to stabilise our stomachs.

'Would you believe I actually toyed with the idea of smuggling an X-ray machine on board?' Cathy smiled. 'Unfortunately it was so bulky it would have sunk *Miss Lucy* within minutes, which you might have noticed. I guess we'll have to manage with the local facilities tomorrow.'

I was glad to see the smile on her face; in a strange sort of way, it seemed to signal the official end of the emergency. We sat peacefully for a while, resting, talking, dreaming, re-living the events of the day, basking in the overwhelming sense of relief that comes from being solidly moored in a safe haven after a turbulent crossing.

Just as I was getting up to clear the table, I heard the sound of two big, throaty turbo-diesel engines ticking away close by. I looked at Cathy.

'Busy place,' I said. 'Do you think this boat is departing or arriving?'

'Can't see why anybody would want to leave in the middle of the night. On the other hand, I'm not sure how they'll squeeze one more boat in?'

'God knows.'

I went up to the cockpit. Sure enough, totally dark except for her navigation lights, a biggish motor yacht was hovering some twenty yards away. The harbourmaster was busy moving a couple of launches to make the last few inches between us and the corner wall available.

'I bet they'll try to squeeze him in next to us,' I said. 'Better check that all fenders are at the correct height: it's going to be bloody tight.'

While Cathy re-organised the fenders, I tried to make out the shape and size of the incoming boat. I recognised one of those Taiwan-built so-called trawler yachts, probably some fifty-five feet in length, that tend to be quite wide. There seemed to be little activity on board, and for the best part of ten minutes the shadowy boat just sat there, her engines idling in a low growl. I thought I could see one lone silhouette slowly going round the side decks, taking ages to fix to the teak handrail what seemed too few fenders. Indeed, much to my chagrin, the boat had only two fenders on our side by the time she slowly began to reverse towards the narrow space between the corner wall and us. I still could see neither her flag nor anybody on the aft deck, where you would expect a crew member to stand at the ready, boathook in hand, waiting to get within range of the mooring line. It seemed that most of the crew had turned in for the night, expecting a man-oeuvre that realistically demands a crew of at least two, and ideally three people, to be performed by the lonely figure whose shadow was now visible on the flying-bridge. I noticed that the harbourmaster, probably exasperated by the time the approach was taking, had disappeared; I assumed he was by now snoring in his office. The motorboat's port quarter was now making contact with our biggest fender and pushing us gently sideways together with the next three or four yachts on the other side. I had to grant the lonely skipper full marks for his boat handling. Everything happened extremely slowly, as it should; he used the absolute minimum of power and kept his boat perfectly lined up, which, admittedly, wasn't too difficult given the absence of wind. I suggested to Cathy that she took his lines ashore and was on my way down below when I noticed the smell. First I thought that it came from our own fetid saloon; but as I turned around and moved on to the deck I realised my mistake. It was a faint but distinctive smell, redolent of the stench I once encountered near a poorly refrigerated Tunisian fishing vessel at the end of a sultry day; the nauseating, sweet and sour perfume of flesh beginning to rot, bacteria at work, decomposing proteins. It could have wafted in from miles away, maybe from some fishing boats moored further along the quay; yet it seemed slightly stronger on our starboard side, next to the open portholes of the newly arrived trawler yacht. I detected a slightly acrid barbecue component in it and wondered whether the crew had indulged in a spot of fishing, or perhaps a number of the passengers had been seasick, which would explain the ship's sepulchral quietness as well as the short-handed crew. As I turned around, heading for my bunk, the skipper came down the ladder from his flying-bridge. For the first time I could see him almost clearly in the light of a lamp-post. He was of medium size and build, wearing a heavily stained whitish short-sleeved cotton shirt and navy-blue cotton trousers, with a flat sailing cap on his head. He slowly descended the five rungs of the teak ladder leading to his aft deck, then turned around and, stooping slightly, walked with leaden steps towards the stern, from where he could see Cathy ready to catch his warps. First I attributed his uneven gait to exhaustion, then – though I could hardly believe my eyes – saw that his right arm was in a sling. On the face of it the coincidence was improbable; never before had I injured myself seriously on a boat, nor had I ever met casualties on other boats. Two arms in slings were more than one would expect in a lifetime. On the other hand – so to speak – the storm had been both unannounced and ferocious, and there was no telling the number of boats it had mauled. What I still could not understand, however, was why the rest of the crew would leave an injured man to manoeuvre all by himself – unless, of course, they were in a worse way themselves. But that sounded implausible, if only because they would then have radioed for help, and the quay, instead of being deserted, would be crawling with doctors and ambulances.

Alternatively, there might be no crew; ill-advised though it would be, a professional skipper might attempt to drive such a boat over short distances by himself. At the first attempt, the line he threw to Cathy with his left arm fell short, so that he had to pull it in again, one foot at a time. By then Cathy had understood that he was injured.

'Hello! Would you like me to come on board?' she called.

'That won't be necessary,' he replied in a low, guttural voice. 'Here it comes.'

This time his throw was perfect. Cathy grabbed the line before it hit the ground and made it fast on the bollard which already held our own warp. As she got up, I could see that she was looking at her hands under the lamp-post. Then she discreetly smelt them.

'Excuse me – I think you are bleeding,' she said to the man as he prepared to throw the second line.

He threw the line without reply.

'I thank you very much,' he said as Cathy got up again. 'You have been very helpful.'

'Look, I am an English doctor,' she said. 'You can't go on bleeding like that. I'd be happy to have a quick look at your hand, if you wish.'

44

Even from a distance, I too could see that, on the spot where he had been standing for only a few minutes, bloodstains were rapidly spreading out. Since I had been unable to help in the manoeuvre, I expected the wounded skipper to assume that I was an ill-mannered wimp, and stayed in the background.

'Have you any kind of proper dressing on board?' the man asked.

'Yes,' Cathy answered. 'I should at least be able to stop the bleeding till you get to hospital.'

'You are exceedingly kind,' he said with the slightly metallic accent that I still couldn't place. 'I am sure that you also had a very long day.'

'No problem. We're not expecting to get much sleep anyway. Just hop on board when you are ready.'

'I won't be more than a few minutes,' he replied before wearily turning away.

Almost immediately, the deep bass of his underwater exhausts stopped, leaving us in the midst of a lingering cloud of noxious diesel fumes that momentarily masked the acrid smell. Cathy went down below to retrieve her suitcase of emergency medical supplies, while I prepared some coffee. True to his promise, our neighbour was already calling from the gangway as I was getting out three cups and still looking for dry biscuits.

'Come in!' I shouted back. 'Welcome on board *Miss Lucy*, the well-known hospital ship. This is Cathy, our medic on duty, and I am Terence J. Garfield, legal director.'

'Kurt,' he announced with a stiff little bow.

Before I could ask whether he was German, Lucy screamed. Cathy rushed to the cabin. Shrieks of blind panic pierced bulkheads, coach roof and my eardrums for several minutes, interspersed with sobbing and panting noises. I wanted to go and hold her, but was reluctant to leave Kurt on his own; besides, there really wasn't room for two adults by Lucy's bunk in our tiny cabin. I could hear Cathy chanting softly as she tried to wake Lucy up or calm her down or send her back to sleep – or whatever. Between screams and heavy sobs, Lucy was trying to speak; but the only words I could identify were: 'I want . . . the Mer-King . . . please, Mummy . . . the Mer-King . . .'

'What's the matter? Are you all right, Cathy?' I cried.

'I think it's only a nightmare,' she called back. 'But she seems to have a high temperature too.'

'I see you have children on board?' Kurt asked hesitantly. 'I can come back tomorrow if that's more convenient.'

'It's only our daughter, Lucy. She's having a nightmare. Unfortunately we got caught in a bit of a blow today, and she banged her head badly. Cathy will be back in no time.'

'She . . . banged her head?'

'Yes. But it could have been much worse.'

'How old is she?'

'Five. Sorry, she's just turned six.'

Kurt stared at me in apparent disbelief, then shook his head, mumbling, '*Ach Gott! Ach Gott!*'

'Do you have children?' I asked.

Again he looked at me uncomprehendingly, as though the question were either offensive or absurd.

'Any kids at home?' I repeated. It was a stupid thing to say since he must have understood first time and was clearly too old still to have children at home.

'No,' he answered in a tone indicating that the topic was now closed. Suddenly he looked distraught. 'I think I'd better put my hand in your sink,' he mumbled.

Blood was indeed beginning to drip from his soaked bandage on to our teak and holly floor.

'Don't worry,' I replied. 'At least it's not a carpet. This teak is quite easy to wipe clean. Not even blood will stain it.'

Nonetheless he placed his right hand in the stainless-steel sink. He seemed to be slightly tottering on his feet, so I assumed that he needed some support. The pungent burning smell I had noticed earlier now filled our small saloon.

As far as the eye could penetrate his greyish three-day stubble, Kurt seemed oddly ashen-faced beneath his mariner's suntan. My first impression was that he had blue eyes, but I soon corrected it. From aquamarine and steel-grey on the outside, his irises imperceptibly shifted towards a lavender hue warmed up by tiny amber specks near the pupils. The combination of these widely spaced and deeply sunken eyes, lightly marked eyebrows and slightly upturned nose made his face look somewhat childlike. However, the wrinkles at the corner of the eyes, the furrows on the vast forehead, the square jaw, and the short, thinning grey hair, all lent him an air of quiet authority. His broad, slightly hunched shoulders and powerful torso seemed out of proportion with the shortish legs. He was wearing a pair of well-worn navy-blue deck shoes.

Suddenly I realised that my last words, still hanging in the air, might be taken to mean that mopping large puddles of human blood from our teak floor was a regular drill on board *Miss Lucy*.

'I never understood the current fashion for deep-pile carpets on boats,' I added to break the awkward silence. 'You wouldn't believe the chaos in this saloon earlier today after that thunderstorm hit us. Pandemonium. Everything on the floor. No carpet would have survived it. Hence the revolting smell – in case you're wondering.'

He nodded gravely.

'We were lucky to escape the worst of it,' he said. 'I could see the thunder and lightning on my port side, twenty miles or so to the west. It looked awesome.'

'What sort of winds did you get?'

'Oh, I guess it blew a force six or seven for an hour or so. In fact we suffered more from the swell that followed it than from the actual blow.'

I noted he referred to 'we'.

'So you were coming from the south?' I asked.

He nodded.

'Where from?'

'Actually, we've been at sea for a couple of days, and zigzagged a few times. Kept changing our plans.'

That settled it: no sane skipper would go to sea for two or three days and nights on his own.

'I'm sorry I couldn't help with your mooring lines,' I apologised, pointing at my left elbow. 'As you can see, I'm slightly handicapped myself.'

'Self-evidently. But the doctor was proficient,' he replied.

'I was slightly surprised that your crew or passengers would let you deal with the mooring manoeuvres all by yourself,' I said. 'I mean, with your injuries.'

He stared at me for a while, his gaze absent-mindedly fixed on the top of my head.

'They had no choice,' he muttered.

I waited, but nothing more was forthcoming.

'Why not?' I finally asked.

There was a pause.

'Why not?' he repeated, before pausing again, as people do when their thoughts are not fully engaged in conversation. 'Why not? Because . . . they are dead.'

Assuming I had misheard, I looked at Kurt with raised eyebrows.

'Can't you smell them? Two rotting cadavers – that's my crew,' he continued. 'Why I, the guilty one, should have been spared – *weiss nur Gott*.'

2

A cloud of toxic silence descended on *Miss Lucy*. It seemed that Cathy had succeeded in calming our baby and putting her back to sleep. When she stepped back into the saloon, I was still gaping at Kurt, wondering what to make of his revelation. Had he just admitted to killing two people? If so, who had 'spared' him? At any rate I assumed that, given his injury, he was unlikely to be dangerous. Frankly, I could have done without any of these complications. Christ knows, we had enough problems of our own. And we needed to rest.

'She's asleep now,' Cathy whispered. Then, before I could attract her attention, she turned towards Kurt, pointed at the settee, and added: 'I'm sorry. Why don't you sit down?'

'May I?' Kurt asked as he grabbed the tea-towel hanging next to the sink and wrapped it around his hand.

'Of course,' Cathy replied. 'You can also have this if you want.'

She retrieved a large plastic bowl from the locker underneath the sink and put it in front of the patient.

'We'd better have a look at that hand of yours,' she said, sitting next to him with her medical bags. 'Does it hurt?'

'Does it hurt?' he repeated reflectively. 'It hurts. Like hell.'

I shifted my weight from one foot to the other, wondering how to warn Cathy, in front of the interested party, that she was just about to treat a double murderer.

'Cathy,' I started, 'it seems that Mr Kurt may have much bigger problems on his hands.'

Kurt looked up at me and palpably tensed.

'Terence, you know where the painkillers are,' Cathy said. 'Do you think you could . . .'

'Of course,' I replied, relieved to have something to do. I'd have to wait for an opportunity to talk to Cathy alone. According to the ship's clock, it was almost two in the morning. 'Forgive me if the service is a bit slow,' I added, trying to reintroduce some levity to proceedings. 'I'm afraid I might be even more cack-handed than usual.'

'I know . . . poor darling! How's the arm?'

'Pretty lousy. At least it isn't bleeding. What was the matter with Lucy?'

'I don't know. She's quite agitated, with a racing pulse and a slight fever. Her blood pressure is steady though. Her reflexes seem normal, and her pupils are reacting well to light. Perhaps we'll have to change our plans and take her to hospital after I've finished with Kurt.'

Since popping tablets out of their plastic wrapping is best performed with two hands, a feat of which only Cathy was currently capable, I handed her the box and put a half-full glass of water in front of Kurt. With this extra casualty, I was going to propose that we all rushed straight to hospital there and then but Cathy had already begun unravelling the thick makeshift dressing of handkerchiefs, towels and rags that bound Kurt's right hand. He swallowed both tablets in one gulp.

'By the way,' Cathy asked him, 'how much water have you drunk today?'

'Not a lot,' he replied.

'What with the heat and your loss of blood, you must drink,' she instructed. 'Terence, do you think you could find a glass of mineral water for Kurt? I think the two bottles in the fridge have survived.'

In no time I brought Kurt his order. First he took only a couple of sips. Then, within seconds, he picked his glass up again and finished it. I refilled it.

The more Cathy peeled off, the less identifiable the remaining pieces of cloth became, half-melted in dark, clotted blood as they were. It was clear that, in order to try and stem the haemorrhage, Kurt had been adding layer after layer over a considerable period. The smell of charred meat was now overpowering. Kurt was silently staring straight ahead at the porthole behind which his floating graveyard of a ship lay hidden in pitch darkness. He made no sound, but the unnatural stiffness of his neck, the twitching muscles of his clenched jaws and the rapidly multiplying beads of perspiration on his forehead betrayed that he was in agony. He looked so utterly drained that I wondered whether there was enough blood left in him to irrigate his head.

'Oh my God! . . .' Cathy exclaimed under her breath as, more liquid than solid, the last layer fell into the bowl.

Thank God I have never been overly squeamish about blood. Strangely, Sarah popped into my head, dainty Sarah who's quite capable of fainting at the mere mention of blood – but I must stop thinking about Sarah.

I had, after all, unflinchingly attended – no, participated in – the birth of Lucy, messy business though it was. But this . . . *this* was something else.

What appeared wasn't a hand. A burnt rump of a hand, at best. I had instinctively looked away; yet the vile image of this stump, this black, incinerated and incomplete appendage persisted long enough to make me feel nauseous. I was almost sure that several fingers were missing, but my eyes hadn't lingered long enough to register which ones. Now, many sailors have lost fingers on boats, which is hardly surprising, given the number of ropes, chains and steel cables on board; but this wasn't the clean injury or neat cut that one would have expected from a sailing accident. It was, from the wrist down, a mangled, charred mess, from which a dirty liquid was oozing on to the sodden cloths piled up in the salad bowl.

'What happened?' Cathy asked softly.

It took such a long time for Kurt to focus on the remnants of his right hand that he seemed to be returning from another, very distant universe.

'Burnt,' he answered.

'Burnt? . . .' I repeated.

There was no trace of fire on his boat. Even if, somehow, he'd burnt his hand on a hot pipe in the engine-room, how could the result have been so devastating? *Exhaust problems*, I thought. Maybe an internal exhaust fire. These things happen. Or perhaps his exhaust mufflers exploded? That's the only way you could get burnt so badly.

'Herr Garfield,' he said, slowly turning his head towards me, 'you carry flares, don't you?'

'Of course. I think I have six parachute flares, four red hand flares, four white hand flares and two orange smoke flares.'

'So you are in full compliance with the regulations. Very wise. Have you ever fired one of those?'

'No. But I certainly wouldn't expect to lose my hand if I did.'

'Do you know at what temperature most of these rockets and sparklers burn?'

'Pretty high, I should imagine.'

'About 1,800 degrees Fahrenheit.'

'Are you saying that all flares are unsafe?'

'No. If properly used I reckon they are reasonably safe.'

I couldn't make sense of his answers. Flares are used by craft in distress as a means of attracting attention. A parachute flare, for example, will shoot up to an altitude of some three hundred metres and glow like fireworks as it drifts down over several minutes. They are potentially dangerous items, which, if misused, can maim the launcher as well as kill anybody in their way. However, not only would Kurt have known that, but his craft seemed totally seaworthy: why fire any distress flares?

'This is going to take a bit of time,' Cathy said. 'The wound to the palm of your hand has probably been sterilised by the burn, but I guess that the rags you put on it were anything but sterile. Besides, the severed fingers clearly haven't been cauterised, or they wouldn't be bleeding so much. I need to clean it and put a dressing on it that will stop the bleeding.'

'You are very kind,' he replied.

'This will take some time,' she repeated. 'Do you want to tell us the story? Perhaps my husband has now sufficiently recovered to make us some coffee.'

'Of course,' I said, jumping to my feet. How could I discreetly tell her she'd just asked a serial killer to confess? Hardly possible with Kurt sitting inches from her. I had to wait until either one of them moved. I wondered whether he'd take up her invitation to tell his story. People do talk to Cathy. She is a listener *par excellence*, always ready and willing to soak up the miseries of the world.

'So?' Cathy persisted gently. 'What happened?'

I think she really wanted to distract him from the cleaning job that she was about to perform on his hand.

'You . . . really . . . want to know?' he asked, looking straight into her eyes.

'Yes, please,' she answered quietly, holding his gaze.

'It is no pretty story. And it is not short. I mean . . . the end makes no sense without the beginning.'

'Isn't that the case with most stories?' she asked, delicately swabbing some blackened scrapes of flesh. 'But it's up to you.'

Suddenly Kurt turned to me.

'Did you say you were a lawyer?' he asked.

'Yes.'

'What kind of lawyer?'

'I'm a criminal lawyer.'

'Please?'

'I'm a criminal lawyer. I defend criminals.'

He reflected for a moment.

'Perhaps you can advise me?' he finally said. 'But I hesitate to request even more assistance from you, after everything you've done already.'

Cathy looked up, surprised.

'It depends,' I replied. 'My firm only deals in English law. But we have correspondents in many countries.'

And that's how I came to hear Kurt's story. To this day I still don't know exactly why my life changed so radically on that night. It may be that the events in themselves would have been enough. I suspect, though, that his tale was a necessary catalyst. What is certain is that I emerged from that endless, short, stinking night a different man. Almost . . . somebody else.

When Kurt started speaking in his monotonous, guttural voice, he was again staring straight ahead at the dark porthole. It was a curious listening experience, for he had a strange, almost hypnotic power of speech. Despite his peculiar voice pitch and German accent, his English was almost faultless.

'My name is Kurt Brod,' he began diffidently. 'But I was born Werther von Ringsburg.'

He stopped. Cathy and I waited.

'My mother was an incurable romantic, and my father had no part in naming me, since he died in March 1945, three months before I was born.'

I looked at him incredulously. I had been expecting a story starting yesterday lunchtime, not fifty-seven years ago. I only wanted to know how his two passengers had met their death. Cathy was concentrating on her patient's hand, waiting for him to continue.

'My father captained one of the last U-Boote to be sunk in the Second World War,' Kurt went on. 'In the first three months of 1945, more or less disobeying orders, he concentrated on trying to protect the ships that were evacuating thousands of refugees out of East Prussia in front of the advancing Red Army. It was an unequal struggle. At the age of twenty-eight, my mother was left widowed with a newborn son amongst the rubble of Hamburg. She was destitute. Of course her story isn't unique; far from it. I'm only mentioning it so that you understand how I became a seaman in spite of her. She had a will of iron, and was determined to provide for me. Her own mother was English, so my mother grew up bilingual; she even managed to teach me English before I was ten. Thanks to her languages, she got a first job as a secretary-cum-interpreter with the British occupation forces. Whenever necessary she would take on whatever menial night job was available in order to make ends meet. Despite an abundance of suitors, she never remarried. I was her world. She was mine.'

Kurt winced as Cathy cut loose some charred tissue.

'Sorry, sorry,' she said. 'Nearly there. Your mother . . .'

'My mother wanted me to lead the free, happy and fulfilling life that had been denied her husband. Only on one point were our views implacably opposed. According

57

to her, my free and fulfilling life was to be a landlubber's. However, the von Ringsburgs have a proud family tradition as naval officers and, from the age of four or five, I knew that my life would be spent at sea. My mother would have none of it. She'd die rather than see her only son pursue any kind of military career. I could obviously have joined the merchant navy, but it did not appeal. I needed more freedom, more adventure. In my teens I also did a lot of competitive sailing, and even won a couple of international regattas. This made me realise that there was a third option, one that offered variety as well as good money. In the mid-sixties, the pleasure-boat industry was taking off, and I eventually persuaded my mother that, if her son became a seafarer, at least he would be safely ensconced on board luxury yachts, as opposed to ducking depth charges in a submarine. We had resolved our conflict. As soon as I passed my *Abitur*, I began my formal training as a *Yachtkapitän* and started work as a deck hand on the sailing yacht of one of the German hereditary steel magnates. The day I received my first pay was the happiest in my life, although I got very little change from the bunch of exotic flowers I bought my mother with it. Am I boring you?'

Cathy and I both looked up, surprised by the interruption. Cathy was making good progress in cleaning his wound, around which large pinkish areas were now visible where charred skin was previously hanging loose. She had to proceed with the lightest of touches, and I noticed that she modulated her swabbing according to Kurt's breathing – or vice versa.

'Not at all,' she answered. 'I've almost finished with the cleaning. I'm sorry it's been so painful.'

'Could I have more painkillers?' he asked.

'I suppose so,' she replied hesitantly.

This time she only gave Kurt one tablet.

'Wait a minute,' she said. 'I need your arm to check your blood pressure.'

Kurt nodded.

'Is your mother still alive?' Cathy asked, fumbling in her bag for her blood-pressure kit.

'No. She died years ago. Alone.'

'Were you at sea at the time?'

'No.'

An awkward pause ensued, during which Cathy listened to his heartbeats through her stethoscope.

'It could be worse,' she announced, putting her kit back into her bag. 'But it could be better too.'

With his left hand, Kurt raised his glass and swallowed the pill.

'Shall I go on?' he asked. 'You must be very tired.'

'Do go on,' she answered. 'I just need to wrap your hand up in sterile dressing, put it in a sling, and then you'll be on your way to hospital.'

'My career progressed very fast,' he resumed. 'Within two years I was first mate on that sailing boat. By the age of twenty-five I was skippering various smaller sailing and motorboats. Because of my languages, I was much in demand. The sort of people who spend time on super-yachts belong to a cosmopolitan jet set, and it is crucial that the crew can communicate with the passengers. At thirty I felt I had arrived. I was captaining *Hot Property*, a 22-metre, state-of-the-art motor yacht owned by an English City type. The owner, Henry Pidgett, and his wife Camilla were only a couple of years older than me. As far as I could find out, he'd made his fortune wheeling and dealing in real estate. *Hot Property*'s crew was quite small for a yacht of that size: there was only Tony, my mate, Katharina and I.

'I had met Katharina on board my previous ship some three years before. I was then skippering this sixteen-metre traditional wooden sloop; she was in charge of catering and accommodation. We immediately fell in love. Orphaned very young, she was passionate about the sea, and had been working on boats since she was a child. Most of the girls who work on boats do it for a bit of fun and a chance to mix with seriously rich people – but not Katharina. Like me, she physically needed sea and salt. She soon developed the skills required to repulse the constant assaults of the spoilt scions who invariably assume that the stewardess should feel grateful for their drunken attentions. I suppose most young women can turn heads simply by exposing enough suntanned flesh on the deck of a super-yacht – but Katharina was in a different league. She could turn heads wearing a diving suit on a moonless night under fifteen metres of water. She was that beautiful. I worshipped her. We married within a year, and afterwards looked for employment as a couple. Tony, the third member of our crew, had come with the boat. He was about twenty years older than us, a bit of a plodder, but solid and reliable, and we all got on well. If required, Katharina was able and willing to give a hand on deck, and neither Tony nor I were bashful about helping her whenever we had a full complement of guests. Henry Pidgett was certainly getting good value from his crew. His wife, Camilla, couldn't have been more charming, as shy and polite as her husband was abrasive. Despite her huge brown eyes, she was no Miss World, but she was kindness personified. Between them, the Pidgetts managed to produce the most delightful little girl. We all adored Rose-Anne, and she ruthlessly took advantage of us. You know how it is with children.'

Cathy and I exchanged a mischievous glance. It was a standing joke between us: I accused Cathy of lacking authority and always relying on me to enforce any kind of discipline, a charge she denied adamantly whilst arguing that Lucy had wrapped me around her little finger. Of course I adored Lucy; maybe, deep down, Cathy feared a rival? This reminded me that perhaps I should go and check on my little girl, but I knew that, having just drunk a cup of hot coffee, simply getting up and moving a few yards in the stifling atmosphere of the boat would be enough to make me sweat profusely. Furthermore my watch alarm hadn't gone off yet. I also didn't want to lose the thread of the story. Kurt had been living the fascinating life which most amateur yachtsmen secretly envy, getting paid good money to pursue his hobby. Too good to be true?

'In the summer of 1975, Rose-Anne was six. Since her birth, the Pidgetts had spent every summer on their yacht with her. At the beginning, they had taken a nanny with them, in order to concentrate on socialising with their numerous guests, but that was before our time. Since I had taken command of the ship, the guests had multiplied, but the nanny had gone, freeing one berth. This suited Katharina and me, since we ended up largely looking after Rose-Anne. Don't get me wrong: her parents adored her and in no way neglected her; but, most of the time, they had to look after two or three couples, friends, business relations, clients, you name it. Cocktails were served from six o'clock, followed by a four-course cordon-bleu dinner prepared by Katharina and Rose-Anne. At least that's what our little girl happily believed. Katharina was delighted to have her in the galley, and managed to keep her amused and interested without slowing down. Rose-Anne also took her dinner and breakfast with us. Every other day, the Pidgetts and their guests would have dinner ashore, at whatever fashionable restaurant might be within reach; our duties then would be limited to ferrying them back and forth in the tender, so that we'd spend a quiet evening on board with Rose-Anne. Sometimes, depending on the day's schedule, we actually ate with her; on other occasions, one of us just kept her company. After dinner, a lot of drinking, smoking and card games would take place on the aft deck. Katharina would help Rose-Anne into her pyjamas, make sure she'd brushed her teeth, twist her blonde hair into two ridiculously short plaits – Camilla insisted on that – and take her to say goodnight to her parents. Oblivious to the risk of spilling champagne on her mother, Rose-Anne would climb all over her whilst Camilla, pretending to scold her, would burrow her nose deep into her child's neck. Amidst the chorus of admiring guests, Henry would lift his little daughter from her mother's lap, throw her up in the air, give her a peck on both cheeks and tickle her just enough to make her hysterical. It was then up to Katharina and me to take her to bed, trying on the way to calm her down. Our method was infallible.

'Rose-Anne loved stories. I guess all kids do. And both Katharina and I loved telling stories. Between the ship's library, which included the complete collection of Ladybird tales for children, and our own repertoire, we had an almost inexhaustible supply. Over the course of three summers, we'd started with easy stories, such as *The Three Little Pigs*, *The Little Red Hen* and *The Ugly Duckling*, moved through *Sleeping Beauty* and *Little Red Riding Hood*, and were now discovering *Beauty and the Beast*, *Cinderella* and *Snow White*. But, in this fateful summer of 1975, Rose-Anne's obsession was *The Little Mermaid*. You know how children are: they like hearing the same stories over and over again, until they know them by heart, and then catch you out if you skip a sentence here and there.'

For a few seconds, Kurt looked at Cathy without seeing her.

' "Far away in the deep, deep sea there was a place where the water was blue and crystal clear. In the deepest part stood the palace of the Mer-King . . ." ' he recited dreamily.

' "The Mer-King lived there with six lovely daughters and their grandmother. The youngest of them had sea-blue eyes and delicate skin," ' Cathy continued.

For the first time since he'd set foot on *Miss Lucy*, the pained shadow of a smile briefly flickered in Kurt's eyes.

' "Like all mermaids, she had no legs. Instead she had a tail like a fish," ' Cathy went on. 'Such a heart-breaking story! Why do mermaids have to die at sunrise?'

'Why indeed?' he echoed. 'Is it not because men are incapable of returning their love? Be that as it may, if ever there was any tension between Katharina and me it was about who should tell Rose-Anne her bedtime story. I used to argue it should always be me, since Katharina's English accent was definitely suspect. Of course, she would have none of it – nor, to be honest, would our girl. Yes, Rose-Anne definitely was our girl as much as anybody else's during those summer months. She made the fact that we did not yet have any child of our own bearable. Oh, there was nothing wrong with us; we simply couldn't afford it. Pregnancy would have meant that Katharina had to stop work, and we would have been separated: she on land, I at sea. We knew this would happen within a couple of years, and both craved a baby, but were trying to postpone the day that would see us parted. After all, Katharina was only twenty-eight; there was still plenty of time to start a family.

'Fortunately, in our daily jousting for the position of storyteller, I had a secret weapon. Rose-Anne would never accept that the end of a story meant it was time for lights-out; she would nag and plead, charm and fume until another was embarked on. "Please, Sea-Mum! I'm not sleepy yet! Another one! Please, Sea-Dad! Just a short one! Just the beginning!" It was hard to resist when Rose-Anne called us Sea-Dad and Sea-Mum. When she was three, her parents instructed her to call us Uncle Werther and Auntie Katharina, but that was far too big a mouthful for a toddler. We never found out how she'd come up with Sea-Mum and Sea-Dad; I think she probably made it up all by herself. At first her parents were somewhat annoyed, but within a couple of days we all became used to it. Anyway, I had found a way around our Sea-Daughter's reluctance to go to sleep, which was to recite to her *Der König von Thule* – in German. Of course she understood not a word of it, yet it had a magical effect on her; she would instantaneously relax, put her thumb in her mouth and fall into a trance. Only once or twice did I get to murmur the final lines of the poem, but even then it was for my own satisfaction. Accordingly, even when it was Katharina's turn to tell a story, I would more likely than not be called upon to perform my little anaesthetic trick, thus watching Rose-Anne as she went limp and her breathing slowed until her heavy eyelids finally stopped fluttering. I would then sit on her bunk for a few minutes, warding off her nightmares and wondering whether Katharina and I would ever be granted such a beautiful child of our own. Little did I know that the events of that summer would see us condemned to childlessness.

'That year I had convinced Henry Pidgett to leave behind the fleshpots of the western Mediterranean and discover the unspoilt beauty of the Aeolian Islands, for a couple of weeks at least. The nearest marina was Porto-sirena on the Sicilian coast, where we based ourselves for the season. Blessed by beautiful weather, we inhaled the sulphurous funes of Vulcano, pottered around Salina, had a quick look at Filicudi and Alicudi, were treated to a magnificent nocturnal eruption by Stromboli and swam off Panarea. Every time we dropped anchor in a place where the water was blue and crystal clear, Rose-Anne would run to me and ask: "Sea-Dad, are we going to see the palace of the Mer-King today?" Whilst her parents were sunbathing or having their siesta, we would put on Rose-Anne's armbands and guide her towards the rocky shore in search of the Mer-King's palace. She never expressed the slightest disappointment at the fact we never found it; on the contrary, she was eagerly looking forward to checking many more coves and creeks.

'Near the end of that cruise we found ourselves at anchor off the island of Lipari. As usual, I had set my alarm clock to wake me up in time for the early-morning weather forecast. A gale was announced as imminent, force seven to eight from the north-west. Without waiting for Henry Pidgett to get up, I decided to weigh anchor and go round the island to seek shelter in the Rada di Lipari. Although *Hot Property* was too big to enter the small port, we would be perfectly snug, anchored on some fifteen metres of water in front of it. Being on the south-east corner of the island, Lipari would remain well sheltered.'

Kurt glanced at me to see whether I was following.

'Makes complete sense,' I said. 'We've anchored there ourselves on a couple of occasions. Not the best place for swimming, as the water is not so clean, because of the boat and ferry traffic; but a convenient place to victual. Or just visit the town of Lipari.'

'Indeed,' he replied, looking at me as though taken

aback by this wholly unexpected rational spark in an inferior life form. 'Too deep and too dirty for swimming. This was a factor. You know how small, apparently unrelated facts and events, innocent in themselves, together lead to an inevitable outcome? As accident investigators well know, the final link is often no less trivial than the earlier ones – only more visible.

'Usually, Rose-Anne had a swim as soon as she woke up, while her parents were having breakfast. Most of the time it fell on me to keep an eye on her and help her to climb on to the swimming ladder when she'd had enough; my attempts to dry her before, naked and quivering with noisy excitement, she ran to her parents, were mostly unsuccessful. I myself had taught her to swim and, being fearless, she was making rapid progress. When she got up that day, we were already under way, so that her morning swim was impossible. "Why are we moving now?" she asked with flashing eyes, biting her lip. "Where are we going?" I explained that we were going to seek shelter from the wind, which was beginning to rise, on the other side of the island. "Sea-Dad, will the water be blue and crystal clear?" she asked. I explained that, unfortunately, the water off Lipari isn't the clearest. "I don't want to go!" she sobbed, stamping her bare foot on the deck. "I want to swim where the water is blue and crystal clear – and look for the Mer-King's palace!" Katharina and I tried everything, but she remained inconsolable, and was still sobbing as we delivered her to the aft deck. Half an hour later, Henry Pidgett appeared in the wheelhouse. He asked whether it was true that swimming had been struck off the day's programme. I explained that swimming off Lipari was perfectly possible, although I personally wouldn't recommend it. "Can you think of any alternative, if only for a quick splash?" he asked. "Rose-Anne needs a swim, but, as you say, there is no point in dipping her in polluted water."

'I had a quick look at the chart. The only coastal indentation between Lipari and us was Valle Muria, near the south-west corner of the island. It is a tiny cove, where I had been a couple of times on smaller boats.'

'I know it,' I interjected. 'But I'd never have thought a 22-metre boat could get in there. And you have to take care of the reef in the middle of it. Sounds dodgy to me.'

Again Kurt looked at me through narrowed eyes and paused for a moment. 'Absolutely right, Herr Garfield. The cove *is* too small. But I knew it well, and I thought we could get away with a quick stop if we anchored near the entrance on five to ten fathoms. We'd be well sheltered from the north, so that the water would be totally flat. I showed Henry the cove on the chart and explained that, though it wasn't quite big enough for us, we might be able to anchor right at the opening – where it was wider – for half an hour or so, before the wind built up any further. At least the water would be blue and crystal clear. He thought it was a brilliant idea and ran to the aft deck to give Rose-Anne the good news.

'By the time we got to Valle Muria a steady force five or six was blowing from the north-west. Given the depth, we'd need to pay out at least fifty metres of chain in order to ensure good anchor holding. As the cove was probably no more than seventy-five metres wide, this meant that we could not drop the anchor in the middle, since, at the end of such a long chain plus the boat's own length, our stern would then have been on the rocks. I therefore dropped the hook quite close to the rocks near the lee shore; within a couple of minutes, driven by the well-established north-westerly, *Hot Property* had backed off and was lying near the other side of the creek, her stern some ten metres from the weather shore. Although she was pulling hard on the chain, the anchor was holding well, and the boat wasn't swinging about. Barring any sudden change in wind direction, which was unlikely given the forecast, the situation seemed reasonably stable. I waited five more minutes, then stopped both engines. As expected, in spite of the increasing wind strength, none of the ripples on the surface of the water were big enough to hamper an average swimmer. First Henry, then Rose-Anne and finally Camilla jumped in and swam towards the shore ahead of us. It was hard going, since they had to fight the surface current generated by the wind, but at least they would have no problem getting back. Slightly concerned that my Sea-Daughter wasn't wearing her swimming aids, I watched them for a couple of minutes and then, leaving Tony on deck, went down to the crew quarter for a quick shave. I would normally shave first thing in the morning; but that day there hadn't been time, what with the unscheduled early departure. How long was I away from the bridge? Maybe five minutes, six or seven at the most. The crew head was a long way down into the bowels of the ship, devoid of porthole and strangely insulated from the outside world. When I re-emerged on deck, Tony was hurriedly starting the engines. Henry and Camilla, standing on a rock, were frantically shouting and signalling to us to manoeuvre away. Although the racket of the wind garbled their words, I instantaneously grasped the situation. The wind had not only freshened, *but veered 180 degrees*. The ship was already lying at a ninety-degree angle to her original axis, and picking up angular speed as the wind swung her around. Within seconds she would hit the rocks *in front of* her anchor, right under the eyes of her distraught owners. We had to swing her back anti-clockwise. Bring the stern back towards the middle of the cove. Fast. I kicked Tony out of the helmsman seat, put the port engine in reverse, and got ready to engage forward on the starboard engine as soon as we'd have picked up sufficient speed astern to move away from the rocks. *Hot Property*'s stern would then swing back towards the centre of the cove with her bow simultaneously moving away from the rocks. Nothing happened. I throttled up to help the boat fight the force of the wind on her beam and heaved a sigh of relief as the yacht first stopped its rotation, then, vibrating under the conflicting demands of the anchor chain holding her bow, the screaming gusts pushing her beam and several hundred horsepower pulling her stern, slowly began to swing back. It had been a close call. Already I felt stupid about having taken such risks.

'It was then that, above the roar of the gale, I heard Camilla's scream. Since I had started manoeuvring, I had neither heard nor paid particular attention to the Pidgetts. Camilla's demented shriek made me realise that they probably had gone quiet during that time – what was the matter now? Before the question was even properly formulated in my mind, I knew the answer. *Rose-Anne wasn't with her parents.* I hadn't seen her standing on the rocks with her parents. *In fact, I hadn't seen her at all.* She must have been in the water. *She must still be in the water.* But where? WHERE WAS MY SEA-DAUGHTER? Since I couldn't see her, she had to be very close – practically underneath the ship. Yelling "She's in the water! The girl's in the water!" I left both engines in gear, stormed past a bemused Tony and ran across the bridge to the port rail. Leaning out further than was safe, I could see the whole length of our waterline – but no trace of Rose-Anne. Another inhuman scream from Camilla made me look up. She and Henry were wildly gesticulating towards the other side of the boat. Camilla threw herself into the water, leaving Henry marooned on his rock. I ran over to starboard. As I peered down at the impenetrable maelstrom whipped up by the wind gusts and our propellers, I still could see nothing. Just froth, foam and ripples. Too much foam. Could my little princess have dissolved into foam already? Then it dawned on me. The boat was now swinging back anti-clockwise. If Rose-Anne had been on this side – the starboard side – she would have been hit by the hard chine of the hull. By now she was probably trapped under the rotating ship. But where? Just then I saw a red speck bobbing up and down. It might have been nothing.

It might have been some piece of plastic garbage, a bottle cap, anything. It might have been the red scrunchie that was holding her hair in place that morning. I yelled at the bewildered Tony to put the engines into neutral. Before finding out whether he'd heard or understood my order, I dived in. Out of the corner of my eye I saw that Camilla was already halfway to the boat. Since Henry wasn't on his rock any more, I assumed he was following her. When I hit the water it felt like concrete. I knew that, whilst underwater, I had to keep my eyes open at all costs, since, as soon as I bobbed up to the surface, I would immediately lose all visibility. I scratched my hands and elbows at the low point of my dive on a scraggy rock that jutted a couple of metres out of the shingles and weeds bottom, apart from which there wasn't much to see – only a couple of inquisitive mullets. I spun around as I slowly rose, trying to investigate a 360-degree horizon. The first thing I noticed was that the ship's hull was getting closer. If Tony had left the engines in gear, she would continue to rotate and land on top of me. Then I myself would be trapped. On the other hand, if he followed my instructions, the wind would probably take her back on to the rocks. I tried to guess what Tony would do, then gave up. Just then it seemed utterly unimportant. My whole being was geared towards finding the six-year-old child who'd somehow been claimed by this aquatic world. But I couldn't hold out one second longer. My lungs were on fire. Before I could spot her I had to re-surface for air. As I desperately tried to catch my breath, my mouth and lungs filled up with the salty taste of betrayal. By then Camilla was only twenty metres away and waving frenziedly. Whenever she could lift a hand out of the water, she seemed to point towards the bow of the ship – unless perhaps she was asking for help. Hindered by the air pockets trapped in my clothes and deck shoes, I swam furiously in the direction she was pointing in and dived again – not very deep this time. I saw Rose-Anne immediately. She was floating at a depth of two or three metres, under the vee of the bow. Gliding towards her, I had the strangest experience. First, relief – naturally. But also infinitely more. Happiness . . . yes absolute happiness. In an anaerobic, blissful trance, I moved effortlessly through the hospitable water. I know it sounds ridiculous – I cannot explain that feeling of fulfilment . . . When I reached Rose-Anne, who was suspended by a halo of golden hair, arms spread out and eyes wide open, she looked straight through me, serene and unconcerned. Her fingers were rhythmically waving in a nonchalant farewell gesture. Fishes swam up to the little girl, letting themselves be patted by her extended fingers. It was then that I made the fatal mistake that was to wreck not only my own life, but also so many others. Instead of taking the hand that my Sea-Daughter was extending and lovingly accompanying her towards the deep – instead, I brought her up to the surface. Brutishly, pitilessly, I dragged her back up to the surface. With terrible foreboding, I then had to swim down the whole length of the ship in order to reach the ladder. As she lay limply against my left arm, my poor little mermaid weighed so little that she hardly slowed me down. At that point I think I half expected her to turn into foam in my hands. Near the stern, I was relieved to hear that the engines were shut down. I didn't fancy having to duck exhausts and propellers. Tony was waiting for me on the swimming platform. He crouched, took the inert bundle from my arms and rushed it to the aft deck. I climbed up the ladder and followed him. Henry and Camilla were already arriving. I'll never forget Katharina's expression as she wrapped the wraith-like body in a multicolour beach towel. I grabbed my little rag doll by her feet, and the towel immediately fell on the deck. Nobody bothered to pick it up. My baby still wasn't breathing. I kept her upside down for a few seconds, in order to dislodge any object or water that might still obstruct her airways. Three or four mouthfuls of water – maybe a glass – poured out of her tiny mouth. I then put her down flat on her back on the aft bench, knelt in front of her and gently started mouth-to-mouth resuscitation. You see, we did not have the luxury of a doctor on board. I was the only qualified first-aider.'

Kurt's last remark had been addressed at Cathy, who had long finished bandaging his wound. Her mouth slightly open, she was sitting transfixed, and I could just imagine what was going through her mind.

'What happened?' she whispered. 'Did you save her?'

'What was I to do?' he asked with a slight shrug. 'She had no pulse. No pulse at all. So I had to start with cardiac massage, whilst trying not to break her ribs. Two breaths – fifteen chest compressions. Two breaths – fifteen chest compressions. And again. Check the pulse every minute.

Start again: two breaths, fifteen chest compressions. I had to be careful not to damage her lungs. As you know, adults' lungs are much bigger than children's; I could easily have injured her by trying to inject into her more air than her lungs could hold. Immobile and silent, Camilla and Katharina, Henry and Tony were standing around us. If they were all praying to their long-neglected gods, it was to no avail. Rose-Anne was slipping away. Her little face was turning a colder hue of blue by the minute. Camilla too seemed to have stopped breathing. She was shivering from top to toe, wordlessly willing her child back to life. Breaking the silence with a low wail, Katharina turned towards Camilla, took both her hands and, slumping to her knees, her head buried against Camilla's belly, started shaking with violent sobs. I don't think I was watching them at the time, I was far too busy; yet, in a state of extraordinary perceptive acuity, I was aware not only of their every move and expression, but also of their thoughts. Or so it felt, until a sudden and murderous anger rose in me. It welled up quickly and powerfully, a holy fury that soon occupied every nook and cranny of my mind. "Take me!" I ordered silently. "Whoever you are, take me! NOT HER!" I threw all caution to the wind and started blowing harder.'

Cathy looked flustered; her breathing was shallow and fast.

'For God's sake!' she whispered. 'Will you tell us what happened to Luc . . . I mean, Rose-Anne?'

'I must have frightened the crazy son of a bitch up there – or perhaps he found the deal irresistible. Two breaths – fifteen chest compressions. Check the pulse again. Every second counted. Deprived of oxygen for so long, the child's brain might already have suffered irreparable damage. Katharina was quietly sobbing at the mother's feet. Camilla was watching the unspeakable horror with such frozen intensity that it was impossible to know whether she was actually seeing anything. Henry was now standing behind her with his arms round her shoulders, his face a silent knot of twisting muscles and deep creases. Two breaths – fifteen compressions. I stopped pushing on Lucy's tiny ribcage and put my ear against her chest. Nothing. Nothing? . . . Weak, erratic, but unmistakable: a flutter. Then – heartbeats. Heartbeats! I stopped the chest compressions and moved to ten breaths a minute, then stopped to recheck her pulse. Still going. Ten breaths. Still going. Rose-Anne, I ordered, start breathing! Now! At first, I wasn't sure whether the movements in the child's torso were simply due to the excess pressure I was applying. But, as I stopped for a while, it seemed that her chest, having expelled my air, was now lifting again – by itself. I watched in disbelief – again it happened. And again. Only when I ordered Tony to put out a MAYDAY call on the VHF radio did the others seem to realise that something had changed. Katharina looked up. "*Sie atmet!*" she murmured. "*O Werther, mein Liebling – Gott sei Dank –* she's breathing!" Camilla dropped to her knees next to Katharina. Suddenly deprived of the support of his wife's shoulders, Henry almost fell down on both of them. I remember thinking that, in different circumstances, this would have been funny. All the while, another part of my mind was trying to compute how long Rose-Anne's brain had been deprived of oxygen. Of course I did not know exactly how long she'd been underwater – but, whichever way one viewed it, it did not look good. At the very minimum she must have spent three or four minutes underwater, maybe much more. Then I must have swum a couple of minutes to bring her back on board, wasted another minute to start mouth-to-mouth . . . how much was that? At least six or seven minutes, more likely ten or twelve. Too long. Much too long. For the first time I looked at Camilla. "She is alive," I said. Camilla did not react. "Alive. She's alive!" I repeated. Camilla still did not move. "May I . . . may I . . . hold her?" she asked in a broken voice. I picked up the multicolour cotton towel that was still lying crumpled at my feet and wrapped the child in it. In addition to the trauma I had inflicted on her chest, I noticed that the small of her back was severely bruised, presumably as a result of her encounter with the hull. I rose, took one step, bent forward and carefully delivered the child's cold body into her mother's shaking arms. "Keep her as warm as you can, face down," I said. "Make sure that everything she vomits drops out. And watch her breathing and heart like a hawk. They might stop again any time." Just then Rose-Anne started spluttering, and Camilla burst into sobs. Realising that she was still wearing no more than a wet bathing costume, Katharina flung another large beach towel over Camilla's shoulders and gently guided her towards the saloon. Henry came forward and started manically shaking my hand. "Well done, Werther. Very well done, old boy," he kept saying. In the background I could hear Tony repeating his distress call again and again, but held no great hope that it would be answered. First it was in English, not Italian; secondly we were far from civilisation. After the twelfth shake I freed my hand from Henry's cold grasp – he too was shivering in his wet bathing trunks – and suggested we go to Lipari as fast as possible. At least there would be a doctor, possibly some kind of cottage hospital. Most importantly we'd find out the quickest way to transfer Rose-Anne to the mainland. Although she was now regaining consciousness, it was obvious that she was in need of intensive care.'

Cathy took such a big breath that Kurt involuntarily stopped and stared at her. I took advantage of the interruption to try and bring the story back on course.

'What damage did your boat suffer when she swung on to the rocks?' I asked. 'Was she still serviceable?'

'In fact the ship never touched the rocks. Tony had only shut down the engines in the realisation that, after a short and aberrant change in its direction, the north-westerly had re-established itself, so that *Hot Property* swung back to her original position.'

'That's amazing,' I said. 'How could such an established airstream have behaved so erratically?'

'Ever heard of katabatic winds?' Kurt asked.

I nodded.

'Then you know how steep mountains falling into the sea can generate force eight winds all by themselves, out of temperature differentials. Well, of course, this wasn't a katabatic wind,' he continued. 'But the principle was the same. Because there are steep hills that fall down into the sea in Valle Muria, and due to the circular shape of the cove, you sometimes get very erratic and swirling winds inside it. At the same time, you might have a very stable airstream only half a mile away.'

'We once spent a very agitated night in one of those supposedly sheltered coves, off Sardinia,' Cathy said. She remembered it only too well. 'Did you find a hospital in Lipari?' she asked. 'What happened to the little girl?'

'We found no hospital in Lipari,' Kurt replied. 'Nor could we get a helicopter. The best we could do was to commandeer the local ambulance boat that whisked Rose-Anne and her parents to Milazzo. She was half-conscious by then, but extremely weak. The next day, they flew back to England on a chartered plane. I never saw that little girl again.'

He stopped and closed his eyes. I waited in vain for Cathy to put the obvious question to him.

'Why not?' I asked quietly.

As though his eyelids were made of lead, Kurt slowly re-opened his eyes.

'Why did you never see her again?' I repeated.

'Because . . . the Pidgetts immediately put *Hot Property* up for sale. Katharina, Tony and I took her back to Portosirena, where we still had a berth for the rest of the season. She felt like a ghost ship. The three of us hardly looked at each other – let alone talked. I guess we were still trying to comprehend what had happened, and worrying about Rose-Anne's prospects of recovery. I was concerned that she had not seemed able to move after coming round, but did not want to alarm the others. Of course they were eaten up by the same unspoken dread, so that even Katharina and I had lost the ability to communicate. We all were on edge, driven to distraction by the lack of news from London. Katharina knew I felt responsible for the accident. I had repulsed her attempts to shift the blame on to events, circumstances or bad luck with such savagery that the whole topic had become unmentionable. Believe me, we were a happy crew no more as, day after day, we absent-mindedly went about our mundane business of cleaning and maintenance. Mind you, the ship had never looked better; all day long, under the hottest Sicilian sun, we vented our frustration on her, polishing her stainless steel, vacuuming her carpets, scrubbing her decks, varnishing her rails and washing her hull. Only complete exhaustion and near-dehydration would make me stop and collapse on to my bunk, in the forlorn hope of snatching a few hours' agitated sleep. Although Portosirena certainly wasn't the kind of trendy marina where you could expect a flow of rich potential buyers, within three months the boat had been sold, probably for a fraction of her value, to some Neapolitan contractor who could not believe his luck. Neither during this process nor afterwards did I ever speak to Henry Pidgett: he made sure that only his lawyer was in touch with us. Our questions about Rose-Anne were left unanswered. The Neapolitan asked us whether we wanted to continue crewing the boat. After some heart-searching, we declined. In truth I felt like scuttling her. That ship was dead. All we could do was to run away from her before she destroyed even more of us. The Pidgetts had never bothered to collect their personal belongings; every picture, garment, book or toy reminded us of happiness destroyed. Every bottle of suntan lotion reminded us of that last morning when we had applied it all over Rose-Anne's lithe body, each brush and comb was redolent of her silky hair. On the last evening, when Katharina came across Rose-Anne's Mermaid pyjamas, carefully ironed and folded in the drawer under her bunk, she finally broke down. She burrowed her face in them and cried and cried until the small hours. It . . . it broke my heart. Yet I had no consolation, nothing to offer her. Nothing. The worst thing was the knowledge that I was responsible for her misery. Her sobs resonated in my head like an accusation, against which no defence was possible. Any effort to console her would have been senseless, since I was the cause of her suffering. No, unless we turned that page and started anew, we would surely go mad.

'When we handed the keys over to an Italian skipper, we left everything behind – except for a couple of children's books and our Sea-Daughter's Mermaid pyjamas. Somehow it seemed wrong that those could fall into indifferent hands. Katharina and I moved into my mother's house in Hamburg and Tony returned to Plymouth, where he came from. I don't know what became of him. After a few weeks, I started looking for work. Only then did the extent of the disaster become clear. Whereas I had previously been much in demand, always in a position to choose between competing offers, it seemed that I had suddenly become unemployable. Admittedly, the boating fraternity was a small, incestuous world; however, I was shocked to find that everybody knew about our misfortune – at least they thought they did. Various versions of the story were circulating, according to which the boat had either been damaged or sunk, the child and some passengers had been badly hurt or killed, and so on. All these stories agreed on one thing only, which was that only a most reckless, incompetent skipper could have been responsible for such a tragedy. As though I carried some abominable virus, old friends turned their backs on me. Whenever I joined a group, at the bar or on the pontoons, conversations died and embarrassed foot-shuffling followed as people muttered excuses and left. At first I tried to put the record straight and defend my reputation, then I gave up. Deep down I agreed with my critics, and blamed myself totally for the accident.'

'But it *wasn't* your fault!' Cathy interjected. 'You were instructed by the owner of the boat to make a stop so that his daughter could swim. Then you were the victim of some freakish acrobatic wind – or whatever you call it. How on earth could you blame yourself for that?'

Kurt was slowly shaking his head.

'I was the skipper,' he murmured. 'I had command of that ship. I was responsible for the safety of my passengers and crew.'

'But accidents do happen, even without human error!' Cathy insisted.

'I did *not* have to stop in Valle Muria. And I did *not* do it as a result of any direct order from Henry Pidgett.'

'What do you mean?' Cathy asked. 'I thought you just said he *did* instruct you to stop so that his daughter could have a swim.'

'I stopped in Valle Muria, I took the risk of anchoring that boat in a cove I knew to be too small, for one reason and one reason only.'

Lost in his thoughts, hunched low on the settee, staring straight ahead at the dark porthole, Kurt stopped for so long that I was just about to prod him when he whispered: 'I couldn't bear it. I couldn't bear seeing Rose-Anne cry. So I indulged her. I irresponsibly, unforgivably indulged her.'

He paused.

'I think you are being far too hard on yourself,' Cathy murmured.

'That's exactly what Katharina used to say,' he retorted. 'It didn't help. Be that as it may, I was more interested in finding out how Rose-Anne was recovering than in defending myself. But all our enquiries into the child's health drew a complete blank. The Pidgetts had neither answered our letters nor taken one single call from me since the day we'd parted in Lipari, and their lawyer seemed determined to erect the most unassailable barrier between them and us. We were ostracised, banished, mercilessly kept at bay. This wasn't the only thing that mystified me at the time. Whenever I followed a lead to find out where a particularly slanderous version of the accident had started, it seemed to have originated in England. This puzzled me, since I thought Tony incapable of any malice – unless perhaps he was trying to salvage his own career by destroying mine. There were even a few articles in yachting magazines, in which, without naming names, the accident was described and attributed solely to gross incompetence on the part of the skipper. Katharina wanted me to sue, but it would have been futile. I only wanted to find out how Rose-Anne was. After a few months, in despair, I hopped on a cross-channel ferry and went to London. Without warning, I rang at the Pidgetts' door. Camilla opened it. She had lost weight and her face was so gaunt that the kind hazelnut eyes seemed bigger. When she saw me, she took a step back and covered her mouth. She didn't invite me in. "Werther! What are you doing here?" she asked. She spoke in a low voice and kept looking over her shoulder. I explained that Katharina and I desperately needed news of Rose-Anne.

' "She'll be all right," she murmured. "Don't worry."

' "Is she here?" I asked, trying to peer past her.

' "No," she replied. Seeing I wasn't convinced, she added: "She's still in hospital. But she'll be coming out soon."

' "What's the matter with her?"

'I heard footsteps behind her.

' "What is it? Camilla, who is it?" Henry called from the top of the stairs.

'Camilla froze. Then, darting another furtive glance over her shoulder, she stepped forward, put her hands briefly on mine and whispered: "You'd better go now. Give my love to Katharina. God bless." Then she gently shut the door in my face. That was the last I heard of her. That was the last we ever heard from the Pidgetts.'

3

Cathy expelled a sigh that sounded almost like a sob. For the last twenty minutes, hanging on Kurt's every word, she had been sitting erect and so still that she seemed to have stopped breathing. His eyes now closed, head inclined sideways, he might have been resting or contemplating. It was close to three in the morning, yet I was feeling sleepy no more; the adrenalin that had accumulated in my body, first during the day, and then when listening to Kurt's appalling account, was still at work. Only when he fell silent did I notice the pain in my elbow; it was getting worse, which made me wonder whether the effect of the painkillers was waning. Cathy got up and slowly started collecting her medical equipment and the plastic salad bowl full of bloody rags that were still lying on the table in front of her.

'Isn't it amazing how those people kept you in the dark about their daughter?' she asked. 'I wonder what on earth was going through their mind.'

Kurt didn't open his eyes.

'I'm going to check on Lucy,' Cathy continued. 'Would anybody like some more coffee?'

'Excellent idea!' I answered. I was acutely aware of the fact that, moving though it had been, Kurt's story did not begin to address the question why the yacht next to us carried two corpses – a fact of which Cathy was still blissfully ignorant. She put the kettle on and disappeared into the cabin. For the first time that night, I detected traces of freshness in the air which lazily wafted in through the open portholes.

'If you will excuse me one minute,' I said, 'I need to take some fresh air on deck.'

Without opening his eyes, Kurt nodded. I began to suspect that he was finally succumbing to exhaustion.

Thankfully, even the stickiest night cools just before dawn, particularly on water. After the confined atmosphere of our tiny saloon, as I stood in the cockpit, breathing in the feeble breeze, the increased supplies of oxygen to my benumbed brain felt like resurrection. The smell from the boat next to us seemed less potent, possibly because the wind was blowing it away. It is funny how the most unbearable stench always seems to dissipate over time, which is just as well, I guess, since otherwise nobody would work in sewers for love or money. Dimly lit by reflections from the roadside lamp-posts, the quay was deserted; not a soul in sight. The only voice I could hear was Cathy's. I figured that she was talking to Lucy and decided to go and see for myself.

'So?' I asked, standing hunched in the doorway at the entrance to the cabin. 'How is the patient?'

Cathy was seated on Lucy's bunk, trying to make her drink a glass of water.

'I had some trouble waking her up,' she replied. 'But you're awake now, aren't you, my darling?'

Lucy nodded and spilled half the glass on to the bunk in the process. In truth, she was a sorry sight.

'Don't worry. I'll get some more,' I said.

When I returned with another glass Lucy, lightly held by her mother, had nodded off again.

'Come on, Lucy. Here's your water,' Cathy said. She turned to me. 'I wish she would wake up properly,' she added.

I raised an eyebrow.

'I'd say she is pretty stable,' Cathy continued. 'But the fever hasn't gone. She's got to drink regularly.'

Cathy gently shook Lucy, who still hadn't stirred.

'Come on, baby – wake up now. You need to drink some more water. Wake up now, darling.'

Lucy obediently opened her eyes and snuggled up to her mother. Then she saw me and – I'm quite sure of it – attempted a smile. Or was it a frown? I brought the glass down to her lips and she took a few sips before making a face.

'Daddy, may I have some Coke?' she asked.

'Of course, my darling.'

When I came back after barely a minute, carrying a can of Coke, despite Cathy's efforts to keep her awake, she had drifted back into sleep.

'There you are, Lucy. Here's your Coke, baby.'

Ever louder, I repeated my invitation a couple of times,

yet Lucy did not re-open her eyes until Cathy gently shook her again. This time she looked quite frightened and her parched lips were quivering.

'Here's your Coke, sweetheart,' I said, bringing the can to her mouth. She pursed her lips, mumbled she wasn't thirsty and fell asleep. I looked at Cathy. She was frowning, a defeated expression on her face as she gently rocked back and forth, holding Lucy against her chest.

'Well, she drank almost a glass of water,' she said. 'We'll try again in one hour's time. I guess we'll have to take her to the local hospital at first light – just to be sure.'

She rearranged Lucy's makeshift head bandages and slowly lowered her back on to the pillows.

'It will soon be dawn,' I said. 'How is the bleeding?'

'Hard to say without taking all this muck off. I guess it's stopped. These stains on the pillow were made by dry blood from the towel, not fresh bleeding.'

I put my hands on her shoulders and started gently massaging them. Rarely had they been so knotted up. 'That's encouraging,' I said.

'If only we could find a half-decent hospital . . .' she sighed. She lowered her voice and continued: 'What are we going to do with . . .?' With her chin she pointed towards the saloon where Kurt was silently sitting, probably fast asleep.

'Well, I suppose he can sleep for a couple of hours, either here or on his own boat, before we find somebody to take us all to the best hospital in town. By the way: don't worry. Your sister was just unlucky with that hospital in Split. This is Dubrovnik.'

'Let's not go into that. What time will it be dawn?'

'Quite soon. This is July, don't forget.'

'Shall we call it a day?' she pleaded. 'I'm just about to collapse.'

'Sure. You lie down next to Lucy. I'll reset my watch alarm to make sure she wakes up fully and drinks in one hour's time.'

She put her hand on mine, which were still rubbing her tense shoulders.

'Thanks – I think I might do that.'

Alone with Cathy for the first time since Kurt had set foot on board *Miss Lucy*, this was my opportunity to share with her what Kurt had revealed to me.

'Cathy, there is one thing you need to know,' I said. 'Kurt told me that he's got . . . er . . . anyway he says he's got two dead bodies on his boat.'

All the tension, all the knots I had patiently massaged out of her neck and shoulders, instantly came back.

'What?' she gasped. '*What* has he told you? Terence, for God's sake, what is going on?'

She had forgotten to keep her voice low. I heard a shuffling noise in the saloon.

'Shushhhh,' I whispered. 'I've absolutely no idea what's going on. I thought he was going to tell us, but instead we had this story about the accident twenty-seven years ago.'

'Forgive me. Nothing is going on,' Kurt announced.

He was standing right behind me.

'So this is Lucy,' he added softly. 'Poor child! How beautiful she is!' Then, after a short pause: 'Why is she wearing these Mermaid pyjamas?'

As I turned around, my hands still on Cathy's shoulders, I felt all the muscles and sinews on her back and neck go into spasm. She shot up from Lucy's bunk, pushed both Kurt and me back into the saloon, closed the door behind her and turned towards Kurt like a fury.

'You leave my daughter alone!' she hissed. 'Like hell nothing's going on!' Then, confronting me: 'Terence, I've had enough. Do you understand? Enough! Let's go ashore – NOW! I don't care whether we go to the police or the customs or the port authorities. There must be somebody in this shithole who can . . . who can take Lucy to hospital and deal with this – this – this German!'

Through a haze of mental exhaustion I tried to work out the different options. Letting Cathy go ashore on her own to explore an unknown city at three in the morning did not sound reasonable. If I went with her, Lucy would remain alone on board with Kurt. This left only one option; however, taking into account Lucy's and my own condition, the prospect of all three of us wandering the streets in the middle of the night was singularly unappealing. Most likely we'd end up mugged in some back alley, or in a police cell trying to explain why we had entered the country illegally. I just couldn't work it out. My brain seemed to have turned into mush. I felt utterly drained; strangely detached too. The only thing I felt capable of was lying down and sleeping.

'Are you listening to me?' Cathy shouted. 'For God's sake, Terence, are you going to do something – or shall I go alone?'

'There is no need to call the police,' Kurt said.

Fast as a rattlesnake, Cathy turned to him.

'Really?' she asked. 'Who says so?'

'They'll be here first thing in the morning. As will the customs. They'll come on board.'

'How do you know?'

'I've been here before. They always do.'

'You know this town? Do they have a decent hospital?'

'I am afraid I do not know,' he answered slowly. 'I have never needed it.'

'Is it true that you have two corpses aboard your boat?' she asked abruptly.

'Yes.'

'Did you kill them?'

'One could say that.'

Looking at me, Cathy shook her head and shrugged her shoulders, as though overwhelmed by the matter-of-factness of the confession. Then she confronted him.

'Are you a murderer?'

'I have killed people. Innocent people.'

Cathy stood silent, staring at him incredulously.

'Was it self-defence?' I asked feebly. 'Did they attack you?'

'You could see it like that,' he answered. 'But I have already bored you far too long with my story. I only did it because I knew that the police might turn up any time, and I wanted the truth to be known before I disappear. But now I must let you rest and return to my boat.' Ashen-faced, he turned to Cathy and bowed stiffly. 'I cannot thank you enough for your kindness. I sincerely hope that your little girl will fare better than mine.'

'Don't mention it,' she replied automatically, as though confused by his politeness. 'I'm a doctor. I was only doing my job. There are no such things as criminals for doctors: only patients. But it seems to me that you were hardly doing your job as a skipper by killing your passengers. Don't you think you'd better tell us the rest of your story? Perhaps Terence can help you if he knows the facts.'

Kurt looked at me. He could see that I was hardly able to stand.

'I have already wasted most of your night,' he said. 'I wish to recommend that we all try to sleep before the authorities arrive.'

'Sleep?' Cathy repeated. 'Sleep? You must be joking. I need to look after my daughter. And I want to know what happened to little Rose-Anne.'

I glared at my wife in disbelief – but she was already in the galley, putting the kettle on.

'At least, let's sit outside in the cockpit, where we'll get some fresh air,' I suggested resignedly as she came back with three mugs of coffee.

So it was that, past three in the Dubrovnik morning, dizzy with exhaustion after the most traumatic day in our lives, we came to hear the rest of Kurt's tragic story. They say it is always darkest before dawn, and I can bear witness: those were dark hours indeed. Yet, no sooner had he resumed than all sleepiness again vanished from my brain. I could see that Cathy too was engrossed. In hindsight, I'd say that his metallic droning produced a kind of reverse hypnosis: it kept us hooked but awake.

'So you want to know about my little girl. And why my passengers are dead,' Kurt started, resting his injured hand on his lap with great precaution. 'I shall proceed as fast as possible. We do not have much time, and nobody else will hear this story. But first I need to tell you what happened to Katharina and me after my inconclusive visit to London. Initially, Katharina was so distraught to hear that Rose-Anne was still in hospital that she decided to go and search all of the children's hospitals in London until she found her. I had great difficulty dissuading her on the grounds that the Pidgetts had clearly decided to keep their child away from us, and that nothing she could do had any chance of improving our Sea-Daughter's condition – whatever that might have been. The hardest thing of course was the uncertainty. It always is. We spent entire evenings debating possible reasons and motives behind the news blackout that the Pidgetts had imposed on us. Katharina thought it might have been in retaliation for the excessive attachment to us the little girl had shown. I sometimes wondered whether it was in order for them to keep control of the official version of the accident, thus absolving themselves of responsibility, or in any way linked to a potential insurance claim. Sometimes the possibility that Rose-Anne had in fact died made Katharina break into hysterical sobbing, but we still couldn't figure out why the Pidgetts would hide it from us. Perhaps, aware of our love for their daughter and of the desperate efforts I had made to save her, they were only trying to protect us? That would have been in keeping with Camilla's kind nature; she certainly would have wanted to spare us the agony of knowing that our little girl had died as a result of an accident on my watch. But this bottomless black hole? This constant uncertainty, the imagining and weighing of endless appalling scenarios, the deafening echoes of our baby's screams, her anguish as she called for her Sea-Dad and Sea-Mum – our uselessness in her hour of need? The heart-breaking visions of her tiny coffin being lowered into some dank dark hole in the ground – of her sitting paralysed in a wheelchair . . . merciless, relentless torture.

'Thankfully, our money was running out so fast that we had to get back to work. I stopped looking for a skipper's position and only sent out truncated CVs that left out most of my professional qualifications and all my recent captain's posts. We took leave of my mother, who never quite understood why we had so suddenly turned up and then stayed in Hamburg; not that it mattered, since, in her old age, she took delight in the unexpected pleasure of our company, and got on with Katharina like a burning house.'

I nearly corrected Kurt, but thought better of it. After all, what's the difference between a burning house and a house on fire?

'Had I known I would never see my mother again,' he went on, 'I might have tried to put on a slightly more optimistic show – been less inhibited in expressing my affection for her. I guess at the time I felt slightly guilty at not having provided her with a grandchild . . . Soon Katharina and I were back to where we'd been five or six years previously; we found employment, mainly seasonal, as a couple, she as a stewardess and I as a deck hand. No, I did not mind. In fact, I don't think I could have coped with the responsibility of skippering yachts full of unpredictable landlubbers at that point.

'For a while it looked as though our lives might revert to an even keel. Then two factors changed that, and I must plead guilty to both.

'First, I started drinking. Unlike many professional mariners, never before had I enjoyed, or indulged in, heavy drinking. This quickly changed. In the evenings, instead of joining Katharina in the crew quarters of whatever boat we might be employed on, I followed my fellow sailors round the watering holes. Soon I was staying on shore longer than them, stumbling back on board only after I'd been thrown out of the last dive. Then I took to stocking a few bottles of whisky in our cabin for those evenings when the silence between me and Katharina was unbearable. I might – God forbid – I might even have hit her on a couple of occasions, when she pleaded with me to stop drinking or hid my bottles. I don't positively recollect it, nor did she ever complain about it; yet, more than once, in the cold light of day, I noticed unexplained bruises on her face. Oh, I was always nearly sober in the morning or when on duty – but never the rest of the time. Needless to say, my jobs never lasted very long. As for Katharina – well, working as a stewardess on rich people's boats is never much fun – even less so when you have to share the few square metres of your cabin with a drunkard. After a couple of years things had got pretty bad. Of course I still loved Katharina more than anything on this earth, but I simply couldn't bear it when she was sitting with a vacant expression on her face, eyes lost in distant contemplation, the corners of her lovely mouth lower than they used to be, prey to the demons that would wake her up night after night, sweaty and screaming, pulse racing and short of breath. I knew that I had fathered those demons – and reached for my bottle.

'Another miserable year went by. Then Katharina decided she wanted a baby. At the time it made no sense to me. Our life was in tatters, we had no stable job and no home. It took me years to understand what her motivation could have been – by then it was too late, far too late. First, we were both over thirty – not old, but in those days it was unusual for a woman not to start her family before thirty.'

Kurt glanced at Cathy, who nodded but remained silent.

'Second,' he went on, 'Katharina may have thought that the responsibilities of fatherhood were the only hope for me. If the advent of a child wasn't going to deflect me from my self-destructive path, nothing would. In retrospect, I guess this probably made sense. But then I thought she only wanted to get away from me. You see, there was no way she could have gone on working on boats during a pregnancy; indeed she was vaguely talking about going back to my mother in Hamburg. In my lucid moments, I understood her perfectly, and only wished she could escape from me before anything irremediable happened. With more alcohol than blood in my veins, it was a different story. Anger took over. I felt betrayed. I also suspected that she was trying to con me into replacing Rose-Anne. Had she actually expressed that wish, it would have been all right: I too needed to replace her. But first we had to agree that Rose-Anne was dead, and bury her. Which was impossible, since it was a taboo subject. And so I grew more and more resentful of what I took to be Katharina's disingenuousness. I understood only too well why, in reality, she may not have wanted a child *with me*. I wasn't assuming her to be in love with me any more. Indeed I sympathised with her. After all, I was just a scumbag, one of so many drunken sailors. But I could not tolerate her *pretending* to want a child with me solely in order to get away from me or satisfy some hormonal drive or surreptitiously replace my Sea-Daughter. I needed her to come clean about it – but never told her so. The dispute simmered for about a year, during which I treated her worse and worse. Of course, she could have had the child against my will, since, few and far between, there were still moments of great tenderness between us, as well as occasional drunken couplings – or rapes, depending how you look at it. She might even have been able to blame it on me. I have often wondered whether she was right in refraining from doing so. Perhaps she could have saved me against my will. But we'll never know what might have been, shall we? We live our life story, others theirs, with no real overlap and no U-turns. Too bad if you miss a turning. Or the only exit. You call it fate, I guess. In German we say *Schicksal*: what is sent

97

us. It rhymes with *Mühsal. Drangsal. Scheusal.* Toil, suffering and monstrosity: that's what is visited on us. *Schicksal* is callous and unconcerned. It is relentless. Apologies. I am digressing again. I beg your pardon.

'By the summer of 1978 we had drifted back to Portosirena in Sicily. We hadn't planned to. I had been sacked from my job on board an American cruise ship and disembarked during her call in Palermo. Palermo being such a smelly dump, it was an easy decision to jump on the Messina train. Within a couple of hours we alighted in Falcone, which as you probably know is the station nearest to Portosirena. We rented a shack in the village at the back of the marina and started roaming its bars and pontoons looking for work. At least it was the height of the season and there was a fair amount of activity. On the third afternoon, Katharina returned to our room and woke me up from my siesta to announce that she had made contact with the crew of a big British ketch that had called into Portosirena to pick up some Italian friends of the owner before a two-week cruise in the Aeolian Islands. They were primarily interested in a cook, but she had persuaded them to take me on as a deck hand, pointing out that I had direct experience of the Aeolians – and that both of us either came as a package or not at all.

'I did not know what to make of it. That Katharina seemed to think nothing of returning to the scene of my crime was mystifying. I wasn't sure I could cope with all the memories that each island, each anchorage, every village and restaurant would unfailingly stir up. After all, we had spent three years trying to shut them all out and move on. Admittedly, they had been unsuccessful years; but how could Katharina even contemplate treading the same waters, let alone do so with apparent equanimity, as though this were just . . . just another job? Was she concealing her feelings, or trying, in some subtle way, to punish me? I told her I would need to see the boat by myself, and would walk to the marina in the evening, after the temperature had gone down a little. "Fine," she replied. "Don't make it too late: they want us on board by 06:00 tomorrow morning. I'll be cooking breakfast for them, and they intend to cast off as early as possible." In the late afternoon, we strolled to the pontoon where the British boat was moored. Because of her size and draught, she was right at the entrance of the marina, opposite the small local fishing fleet, on the same side as the repair yard and the Yachting Club restaurant. She was a magnificent ship, more than twenty metres in length, all mahogany and teak and shiny bronze, immaculately kept and proudly flying an oversized blue ensign as well as the burgee of some exclusive yachting club. A splendid sight, which awakened nostalgic feelings in me. Whoever skippered that ship clearly knew his business and took pride in it. As we walked past her, I was looking up at her masts, analysing the finer details of her rigging. "Hello, Katharina!" a voice suddenly boomed. "Are you all packed up? You can join ship tonight if you prefer!" Two young men were sunning themselves on deck; they raised their glasses in our direction. The man who'd just hailed Katharina was tall and broad-shouldered, fair-skinned and slightly freckled, perhaps because of over-exposure to the sun. He had an open and friendly face, whose square jaw betrayed a natural leader. I couldn't see his eyes, which were hidden behind the double protection of a sailing cap's visor and sporty Ray-Ban sunglasses. "He's the owner's son," Katharina whispered to me. "The one who gave us the job. In fact he's acting skipper on this cruise. Would you believe he speaks German? He says he studied in Hamburg for a year." She took a few steps towards the two men. "Thank you very much, Mr Jones," she shouted back. "I think it will be more practical to stick to the original plan, if you don't mind. This is Werther, my husband." "Hello, Werther!" he yelled. I bowed and decided I had seen enough. As we started on our long way back to the exit on the other side of the marina, both men cheerfully waved us goodbye. "See you tomorrow then!" Mr Jones bellowed. "Don't be late!" Katharina smiled and waved back at him.

' "Shall we sit down and have a drink?" I suggested some twenty minutes later as, moist with perspiration, we reached the bar of the marina. I suspect I really wanted to find out Katharina's true feelings about the prospect of going back to the Aeolians. For my part, if anything, my misgivings were growing by the minute.

' "I think I'd better go back and start packing," she said in a neutral voice. "We won't have much time in the morning. You won't stay out late, will you?"

'Those were the last words I ever heard from my wife. She planted a kiss on my cheek and walked away.

'That evening, I started drinking earlier than usual, and did not stop until dawn. I have no idea how I came back to our room; it may be that one of the waiters dumped me there on his way back home. When I woke up in the early afternoon, feeling worse than death, Katharina had gone. Although this was the first time since our marriage she'd be working on a boat without me, my first reaction was one of relief. At least she'd earn some money, and wouldn't be on my back over the following two weeks, her very presence a silent reproach. More to the point, I had escaped the terrifying prospect of a reconstruction of my crime. I vaguely remember remaining drunk for the best part of that fortnight. At the end of it, I staggered back to the marina and spent a couple of days idly waiting for the English ketch to reappear. When she did not, I fell prey to an irrational terror: the Aeolian curse had struck again, some terrible accident had taken place, and I was going to be punished through the loss of my beloved Katharina. My enquiries soon revealed that no such drama had unfolded around the Aeolian Islands; those who'd come across the English ship reported that there did not seem to be anything wrong with her. Eventually I met a sailor who'd shared a few drinks with her crew in Lipari, and seemed to remember that their next port of call would be Sardinia, on their way to the South of France. Further enquiries confirmed that she had indeed called into Cagliari, then I lost her trail.

'Even then I refused to accept the facts. For several weeks, I deluded myself that Katharina had had to extend her job for a while, due to a sudden change of plan on the part of the owner. Owners are notoriously fickle and don't give a damn about the private lives or convenience of their crew. It would have been difficult for her to warn me about an extension of her tour; there were no mobile phones in those days, and I had no telephone connection at home. She probably hadn't thought of trying to phone or fax the marina office in Portosirena and leaving a message for me. Perhaps she imagined I would hardly notice her absence, or didn't care. How wrong she was! When I realised, in the third week, that she had packed not one bag, but two, and left nothing of her few belongings behind, the discovery shattered me. Nothing, not a sweater, not a single T-shirt, not one dress, no scarf, no handkerchief, no toiletry item. I slumped into the depths of utmost depression. But when, a few days later, I stumbled on some underwear in a laundry basket, it felt like an immense victory, and I started to believe she would return. For several weeks, waiting for Portosirena's erratic postman occupied most of my mornings. Since he had never delivered a single letter to me, he soon assumed, with the infallible instinct of the uninvolved, that I was insane. Seven months – I hung around Portosirena for seven months, waiting for my wife. As soon as the postman had been and gone, I would take up position with my binoculars at the end of the breakwater, at the foot of the green light tower that marked the entrance of the channel leading to the mar-ina. I don't know why I was expecting the sea to restore my wife to me. My attempts to trace the ketch back to Britain failed: she was registered in the name of a Jersey company; as far as finding the right Joneses in the whole of the United Kingdom was concerned – no chance. I got in touch with my mother and asked her to let me know if Katharina ever contacted her; this only served to distress her, and nothing came out of it. I did not dare embark on any boat lest I should be at sea when Katharina reappeared; I became an odd-job man, unblocking sea-toilets, cleaning hulls and polishing superstructures. I stopped drinking. Perhaps it was the shock, perhaps it was the need to be lucid enough to conduct my enquiries – or it could have been the urge to be presentable on the day of her return. Never since have I touched a drop of alcohol. Who knows? Maybe she would have saved me in spite of myself – assuming one can ever be rescued from one's fate.

'The Italian boating season is very short. In fact, it hardly extends beyond the month of August. By the middle of the winter, I was starving and desperate. Katharina wasn't coming back. I had lost my wife, my loving companion, my beautiful and sad lover. I would never know the children she had offered to bear me. Rose-Anne would remain in limbo for ever. This left three options. I could keep waiting and slowly starve to death. I could expedite things and shoot myself. Or I could find somebody else to do it. Before Easter I had changed my name to Kurt Brod and signed up for ten years with the French Foreign Legion. I neither wished nor expected to see the end of that contract. Whenever the 2nd Régiment Étranger de Parachutistes saw action, be it in the Ivory Coast, Congo, Cameroon, Rwanda or any other French fiefdom – I was there. Loyada, Kolwezi, I was there, with the amphibious 3rd Company. Several tours of duty in Chad. Beirut in '82. Gabon. I was there. Leading the charge. Several times I was offered promotion and distinction for "outstanding bravery". I never accepted, since in reality my behaviour only reflected extreme fear – the fear of living. All I wanted was that bullet with my name on it to find its target and put an end to my misery. All that happened is that my *baraka* became legendary. Do you understand *baraka*?'

Surprised by Kurt's unexpected question, Cathy and I both started, before shaking our heads in unison.

'Luck,' he explained. 'I think it comes from the Arabic. It is his *baraka*, for example, that saved General de Gaulle from several assassination attempts. Isn't that ironic? I, most desperate of desperadoes, enjoyed such supernatural luck that all legionnaires in my company insisted on shaking my hand or at least touching some part of my body or equipment before going into action. I never bothered to bend or crawl under fire, walked though minefields looking at the clouds, volunteered for reconnaissance behind enemy lines, dragged fallen comrades back to our lines under machine-gun and mortar fire – and failed to catch that bullet. The sheer incompetence of those mercenaries and so-called rebel fighters! I couldn't believe the way they kept missing me.'

Perhaps because Kurt's love story was troubling me, or possibly because I was beginning to resent the fascination he visibly exerted on Cathy, I suddenly felt the urge to break his spell.

'These mercenaries and rebels – have you ever considered suing them for gross negligence or dereliction of duty?' I interjected. 'It may not be too late, you know.'

'Not funny, Terence,' Cathy said sharply. 'Please don't pay any attention to him,' she told Kurt. As it turned out, the apology was quite unnecessary, since Kurt, utterly unruffled, simply ploughed on.

'No wonder we were able to maintain some degree of order over half a continent with only one regiment. Then, when the old Transall transport aircraft flying us back to our Corsican base ran off the runway in Calvi, killing or maiming most of my platoon, I walked away almost unscathed. One of three unharmed survivors. I was incensed by what I perceived as rotten luck more than *baraka*. Still, that crash was a turning point. Initially, I was filled with resentment at having survived against any reasonable odds; then, I slowly began to realise that I could have been maimed, like so many of my comrades – maimed and alive – the worst possible fate.'

As though struck by a sudden thought, Kurt stopped and pensively stared at the stump of hand lying on his lap.

'I had to accept that it wasn't my fate to die a legionnaire,' he resumed. 'And then I started to wonder. Was there a reason for this state of affairs? Did it perhaps make sense in any way? Part of me wanted to hope that my debt had been repaid in full, that the time for expiation was over – that perhaps life had something to offer, since death was rejecting me. I forgot that between life and death, limbo is vast and grim. How do you say in English? Hope is eternal?'

'Hope *springs* eternal,' I whispered automatically.

'While there is life, there is hope,' Cathy echoed softly.

Kurt meditated for a moment.

'Thank you,' he resumed. 'Perhaps a cliché – but full of wisdom nonetheless . . . Life – indeed. How can men be so wise about their own folly? Why is it that, even when we look ahead, and the tragic end of our story is plain to see, we keep hoping against hope that some impossible event, some *deus ex machina* will deflect its fateful outcome?'

'God knows,' Cathy murmured dreamily. 'Maybe listening to stories would otherwise be unbearable. For example, who wants mermaids to die at dawn?'

'Do you know why children love stories?' Kurt asked.

We waited.

'Because they think it is fantasy. Fantasies are safe. But we adults recognise their unspeakable truth,' he went on.

'Truth? That is a big word,' I interjected.

'What do you actually mean?' Cathy asked.

Kurt pondered for a moment.

'Who is lurking behind all the monsters, witches, wolves, giants and sorcerers? Who, if not man? Cruel, selfish, exploitative man?'

'What about love?' Cathy asked.

'Even when men love they are mostly being selfish.'

'Do you really believe that?'

'Have you forgotten why the Little Mermaid was doomed to die at dawn?'

'Well . . . she dies of love, I suppose,' Cathy murmured.

'That's right,' I confirmed. 'When she goes to the witch early on, and asks to be changed from a mermaid to a woman, the witch warns her: *'The very first morning after the Prince has married another, your heart will break and you will become mere foam!'*

'Right,' Kurt answered. 'And the Little Mermaid gladly takes the risk, because she is in love with the Prince. But why does she then fail to seduce him? Because, in payment for her services, the greedy witch has deprived the poor mermaid of her best possession – her lovely voice. So, you see, it was the exploitative greed of others that rendered the Little Mermaid voiceless. Mute. Hopeless.'

I sensed Cathy tense up and imperceptibly move away from me.

'Perhaps women are more resilient than mermaids,' she said. 'Perhaps we know men better, and expect less from them. We soon learn that they can be selfish and unfaithful.'

During the long pause that followed, I wondered whether I'd heard her correctly. I wasn't sure whether to ask her to clarify her meaning, at the risk of sounding concerned, or let it pass. For the first time that night, I felt relief and gratitude when Kurt eventually resumed his story.

'Where was I? Ah, yes, my last year in the Legion. It was intolerable. Having wasted nine of my best years in such sordid company, I suddenly became obsessed by the fear that, through some supreme irony, the magic bullet would strike just as my appetite for life was being reborn.

Shame also grew unendurable. Shame because I had broken the promise made to my mother all those years ago that I would stay out of the military. Shame because I had allowed myself to be treated like cannon fodder. Shame because during all this time I had had no contact whatsoever with my old mother. I had blithely assumed she would suffer less from my disappearing from the face of the earth than if I owned up to being a professional killer. I was ashamed of having fought the ragbag of truant schoolboys, famished peasants and amateur mercenaries who, armed with machetes and rusty Kalashnikovs, staged bungled coups against corrupt potentates. In order to punish myself I had harmed others – and I despised myself for that.

'After my discharge I took the first flight to Hamburg. I was prepared to make up to my mother, ask her forgiveness and live with her until the end of her days – if she would have me back. Though I wouldn't admit it to myself, I was also harbouring vague hopes that she might have news of Katharina. The nice young couple who warily opened the door of the small house told me they had lived there for some five years. Of my mother they knew nothing, but they gave me the name of the lawyer who had handled the sale of the property. I vaguely remembered Herr Doktor Miersch. His office informed me that he had been retired for some time but gave me his private address. A contemporary of my mother, he was frail and white-haired, as tall and thin and erect as a Sicilian cypress. He told me that my mother had been dead for seven years. "What happened?" I asked. "Did she fall ill?" Herr Doktor Miersch looked at me sternly and did not answer. There was no need to: it wasn't difficult to guess why my mother's heart had finally given up. With a slightly reproving expression, Herr Doktor Miersch said that, together with my mother's personal effects, my small inheritance was waiting for me to claim it, and sent me back to his office with the details of the ex-colleague of his who was now in charge of the file. Sensing that he resented my presence, I left so quickly that I even forgot to ask him where my mother was buried. As I had in life, so I betrayed her in death. I wept – more for myself than for her. I mourned – more the loss of her son Werther than her own demise.

'When it came to news of Katharina, I had drawn a blank. All I'd managed, with great difficulty, was to track down her only brother, who'd moved to Berlin: he said he had no idea of her whereabouts and rudely put the phone down.

'Only when I started discarding my mother's reams of bank statements and utilities bills did I find the two yellowed, unopened envelopes which had arrived in the months following her death.'

'My God!' Cathy gasped. 'Letters from Katharina?'

'Indeed,' Kurt answered. Fumbling with his left hand in the buttoned, bulging breast pocket of his shirt, he eventually produced two crumpled envelopes. 'Here they are.'

'Did she tell you where she was?' Cathy asked.

'The first letter was to my mother. This is what it said.'

Kurt carefully put both envelopes back in his shirt pocket, took a deep breath and started reciting:

'Luanda, 16 February 1983

'Dearest Mutti

'Please, please read this letter, even if you hate me, even if you have decided to cast me out!

'Can you ever forgive me? After all you have done for Werther and me, how ungrateful, how heartless I must appear to you after five years of silence! I am so ashamed of not having visited you for so long! How are you?

'Yet – please believe me! – you have been in my thoughts every day. Thinking of you alone in your old age makes me cry. I can only hope that Werther, deprived of a wife, came back to you, and that you gave each other the support I could provide no more.

'Dearest Mutti, I am so sorry about what happened. I never meant it to. It was only because Werther had shut me out of his life – just as he had shut himself out of it. He had replaced his life – our life – with alcohol. Need I say more? Like so many alcoholics, he refused help. He refused my love. I could have lived with that – but not with the daily sight of his self-destruction.

'Has he ever told you about the accident in Sicily, some eight years ago, when a little girl nearly drowned? This was just before we came back to Hamburg to live with you. If he hasn't, you must try and make him talk about it. I have come to believe it was our inability to talk about it that drove him to alcoholism. The pain! I think that, had he tried less hard to deny and repress his pain, he wouldn't have needed alcohol to blot it out.

'Mutti – I have failed Werther. First, in not finding the words to reach him. Second, in leaving him. There are no excuses. For three years after the accident I did try – to no avail. He was sinking lower and lower. I just could not keep him afloat. In the end I thought that perhaps it would be best for him if I left him alone. Not because he was dragging me down: I would have given my life for him. But he did not want my life. No; I sensed my presence oppressed him. I was a constant reminder of that dreadful accident, and so tried too hard to exculpate him from any responsibility – that simply enraged him. Of course the accident wasn't his fault; it resulted from the unluckiest combination of circumstances. But Werther knew that, as skipper, he was responsible. I also knew he was, but couldn't talk about it. He knew that I knew, but did not want to talk about it.

'Poison.

'But this is all in the past. What matters, darling Mutti, is that I still love Werther. I have never stopped loving him. I never shall.

'Of course I realise that he may have another woman in his life – a woman who makes him happy, perhaps already the mother of your grandchildren. How beautiful they must be! Should this be the case, please burn this letter. Let him forget.

'But if he's alone – if he sometimes remembers his loving Katharina – if sadness darkens his life as it does mine – then let not one second be wasted! Please, Mutti – please – make haste and deliver the enclosed letter to my husband.

'If I do not hear from you, if Werther is still prey to his demons, if he cannot forgive me, I shall pester you no more. Then, pray for me, as I pray for you every day.

'Your Katharina

'P.S. Please tell my brother that I am fine, and send him my love.'

Kurt's flat delivery, in contrast to the tone of the letter, somehow made it even more poignant.

After he fell silent, there was a long pause. It was broken when Cathy asked in a small voice: 'The other letter . . . was it to you?'

'Yes,' he answered. 'The other letter was written in Lagos two days earlier. It read:

'My love

'We all indulged Rose-Anne. Her parents did; I did; even you did.

'That's why she got to swim in Valle Muria that day. You, in particular, overrode your professional instincts out of love for that little girl. That was a mistake.

'There.

'It has been said.

'Had I said it to you five years ago, perhaps we could have moved on. We would have agreed that the Pidgetts bore as much responsibility as we did. Henry did order you to stop – I heard him myself. They all

jumped in the water before you came down from the flying-bridge – without giving Rose-Anne her swimming aids, as you unfailingly did. None of this was your fault. You had anchored the boat with consummate skill; the freakish wind that swung her around wasn't your fault.

'You risked your life to save Rose-Anne. I was proud of you and will remain proud of you till death do us part.

'Werther, my beloved husband, I am sorry. Sorry that, at the time, I couldn't find the courage to tell you that I understood your responsibility – and was proud of you. You were so hard on yourself! I tried to defend you against yourself. To convince you that you bore no guilt whatsoever. That it had been a pure accident. One of those things. But you would have none of it.

'And so, my only love, we lost each other.

'I'll never forget the day I left.

'All night long, as so many nights before and since, I had been achingly aware of your absence. Believe me, awake or asleep, a neglected wife always knows that she's alone in bed. I got up at five, exhausted. You were lying in a pool of vomit, down in our tiny entrance hall. I tried to rouse you, but you were in the deepest stupor, almost comatose, and showed not the slightest sign of hearing me. With unnatural strength, I dragged you into bed, undressed and carefully washed you. There wasn't much time: we had to be on the English ship by six, and still you did not stir. Between my sobs I kept begging you to wake up. I cried in your ears and implored you not to let me go on my own. To hold on to me. Strangely, when you started snoring, I was relieved. Relieved that you were not going to die of toxic shock. Relieved because things had been taken out of my hands. Relieved that there was no alternative.

'The church belfry struck half past five. I quickly crammed nightgown and toiletries into my already packed sailing bag – and then, next to it, naturally, I saw yours. You remember, that huge black holdall with the strange rubbery straps, that you already had when we first met, on the big sailing boat? Never since had our bags been separated. On the contrary, afloat or ashore, they'd lived one next to the other, one on top of the other, one inside the other. No sooner had I thrown half a dozen of your shirts into your bag than I realised it was futile. In a frenzy, half blinded by my tears, crying and shouting at you, I took them out again and threw them back on to your shelf. Then, hardly knowing what I was doing – supplicating, imploring, ordering you to get up – I swept the contents of both my shelves into your bag; and still you ignored me. I tore down my three dresses and stuffed them into your bag together with my winter cardigans and jeans. I stopped to catch my breath. Turned around. Looked at you. Took two slow steps, bent down and kissed you . . . long, long, long and hard. I don't expect you remember our last kiss? Your lips were so cold! Then I carefully wiped my tears from your face – your forehead – your eyelashes – your movie-star's chin – and picked up both bags. How could you? For God's sake – Werther, my husband – how could you let me slink into that grey dawn like an unwanted dog? Childless – childless, orphaned and widowed, laden with a big black sailing bag and a small green one, I stumbled to work. I didn't close the door behind me. Nor did I once look back, lest I stopped dead in my tracks.

'There were seven people aboard Sea Conqueror: Albert Jones, the owner's son, and his fiancée Helen; Jeff and Amanda, two of their friends; Bryan, the skipper, and his wife Nelly; and last, Arturo, the Filipino deck hand. I explained that you were feeling unwell, and wouldn't be joining ship; this wasn't a problem, since they'd initially only wanted a cook. Nelly, a kind middle-aged woman, immediately took me under her wing and helped me carry my bags to my bunk. Within minutes I was at work in the galley, and breakfast was ready well before the passengers appeared on deck. Fortunately we cast off almost at once, before I had time to change my mind and jump ashore. Only two days later, as we were anchored off Lipari, did I break down. I realised that you had been right, that the wound was still raw, and that I couldn't cope with the memories. Having failed to cheer me up, Nelly must have mentioned to Mr Jones that I was in constant tears, for he came to me in the evening and asked what the matter was. I apologised and told him it would soon pass. "Are you missing your husband?" he asked. I knew that if I tried to answer I would start crying again. "You may leave us any time, you know," he went on. "I won't hold you to your contract if you are unhappy. There are daily ferries from all these islands to the mainland. Of course we all would miss you – I think we're already addicted to your cooking. But you'll have to make up your mind soon, before we leave the Aeolians."

'I thanked him as best I could, and resolved to honour my contract. Over the following days, I felt better. Knowing that I could get back to Portosirena at any time helped me stay. After a week we left the Aeolians – and I was still on board.

'By the time we left El Kantaoui in Tunisia Albert knew all about you. Not because I wanted to tell him – or anybody, for that matter – but he soon developed the habit of seeking me out during my rest hour. He wasn't really nosey, or bossy, no; just . . . interested. As he gently prodded, I felt he genuinely wanted to help us. Of course I told him it was neither in his power nor in anybody else's to do so, but he kept saying I should let him try. If ever I was sitting on the foredeck at the end of a day's work, having helped Nelly to clear the table and done the washing-up, he would suddenly appear and we would chat for a while, until his fiancée's strident calls claimed him back. Never did he allow himself the slightest impropriety, though this in no way reassured Nelly. "Be careful, love," she used to say. "The young master means well, but if you let him start, it will end badly." "Nothing will start!" I replied. "I am a married woman, I love my husband, and he's waiting for me!"

'As long as Albert's fiancée was on board, I felt totally safe. Not that she gave any sign of appreciating me; on the contrary, she always seemed to find fault in my cooking, and soon behaved as though she disliked me intensely. Since there was no reason for me to come into contact with them except at meal times, I tried to stay out of the way of all the passengers as much as possible. By the time we reached Cagliari, Nelly reported having overheard a blazing row between Helen and Albert, and the looks she and Bryan gave me were enough for me to understand that they saw me as the probable, if innocent cause. Whenever Albert would join me – he often offered to go shopping with me, arguing that he loved the pungent smells and bright colours of these open markets, and carried all my bags – I tried to run away as soon as politeness would permit. This wasn't always easy since, as you well know, a boat is a fairly confined space, and he was my boss. And – I'll admit it – he was touching in his attentions. Only now, some five years later, do I realise that never, before or after, have I been courted in such a way. With infinite patience and gentleness, with warmth and understanding, without demands. You, Werther, my true love, never had to court me, did you? You swept me off my feet the second I set eyes on you . . . as you would sweep me off my feet today if ever you claimed me!

'What was I to do?

'The thought of returning to you was irresistible – the prospect of finding you in a drunken stupor unbearable. Every day I resolved to disembark at the next port of call, before Nelly was proved right. Each time I shrank back from the vacuum, the frightening nothingness of life without Sea Conqueror, the loss of my surrogate parents, Bryan and Nelly.

'When we arrived in Cagliari for a refuelling stop, I packed my two bags. Your big black one, my small green one. Our next destination was the Balearics. Too far. As long as you were in Sicily, leaving Italian waters felt like betrayal. I asked Nelly to tell Albert I would be leaving the ship that day and to collect whatever wages I might be due. Hardly five minutes later there was a knock on my door. It was Albert, slightly out of breath. Never before had he entered my cabin. "May I come in?" he asked. I moved sideways to let him in. His broad shoulders occupied almost all the space between my bunk and the bulkhead opposite. "Is it true you want to leave?" he asked. Looking down, I nodded. "Katharina, I want you to know something," he went on. "Of course you are free to go. But you shouldn't go on Helen's account. I realise she has been unpleasant to you – I'm terribly sorry. But it won't happen again. As it happens, she's leaving us today, and I don't expect her to come back." He was standing so close to me that he could hardly breathe without touching me. "I am sorry Miss Helen is leaving, Mr Jones," I mumbled. "But I can't leave Italy. Not as long as my husband is here." He looked so dejected that my heart bled for him. "Naturally – that is entirely to your credit," he murmured. "But, by your own admission, your husband has been an alcoholic for years, and you haven't been able to help him. Only your absence might shock him into curing himself. Or so you told me yourself. What's changed?" I thought for a while, then looked up at him. "What would be the point of Werther being cured if he was never to see me again?" I asked. "Katharina," he pleaded, "be realistic. You've only been away a few weeks. If you go back now, you'll be walking into the very mess you tried to leave. Give that shock therapy of yours at least a year. Otherwise you might deprive your husband of his last chance. And you might get hurt."

'Poor Albert. He was so sincere! Trembling all over. Suddenly he took both my hands in his: "Please, Katharina! I know it means nothing to you – but I cannot bear the thought of you getting hurt!" I freed myself gently. "Please go," I whispered. "I need to think it over. I'll let you know tomorrow."

'That night, I did not sleep. My head couldn't fault Albert's arguments, yet my heart was rebelling. At dawn I decided that, in your best interests, I should stay in my floating cocoon. For a few more months.

'I unpacked my bags, rolled up the big black one, put it inside the green one and stowed both of them in the locker under my bunk.

'Helen did disembark in Cagliari. A few days later, the remaining two passengers, Jeff and Amanda, left the ship in Palma de Majorca. Then, much to my surprise, Albert announced that Sea Conqueror wasn't headed for the UK any more, but would winter in the Balearics before heading towards Greece the following season. The uncomfortable thought crossed my mind that perhaps he was trying to humour my desire not to leave the Mediterranean. We remained in Palma for several months. Only the four crew lived permanently on board – that is, Bryan and Nelly, Arturo and I. We all got on happily, and the days passed quietly. My workload was light. I spent most of my time reminiscing about the blissful years you gave me at the beginning of our marriage, and wondering how you were faring. Only when Albert flew in from London was my relative peace of mind shattered. Somehow he seemed able to escape from his obligations two or three times a month in order to spend a few days on the boat. As we walked around the Plaça Major or sat at one of its many terraces, he told me about the domineering father who wanted him to take over his car-parts business. Next to the swimming pool at the Club de Mar he told me about his love of the sea and passion for ocean racing. As we took in the breathtaking view from Bellver, he told me about his years at boarding school – would you believe he was sent away from home at eight? In the cathedral he told me about his few friends and the many children he wanted. Back on board he talked about the plays he had seen, the books he wanted me to read. He explained to me that Helen was the daughter of his father's business partner, and how their union would have kept the business in the right hands. Soon I noticed that his already good German had improved to such an extent that it now bettered my English; when I mentioned it he blushed and confessed that he had been attending night classes at the Goethe Institute in London. Against my express wishes, he always brought me gifts: records, books, scarves and flowers and chocolates that I shared with Bryan, Nelly and Arturo. "Be careful, love. Be careful!" Nelly would sigh in ever more forlorn tones whenever she helped herself to a delicious Swiss or Belgian truffle.

'Once – it must have been very close to Christmas – Albert took me, his cook, to dinner in one of those quaint Cellers near the Llonja in old Palma. Albert never tried to impress me by booking tables in flashy, trendy tourist traps; on the contrary, he was interested in atmosphere and traditional Majorcan cooking. Only after we had sat down, at the very corner table where you and I used to sit on our days off, did I recognise Celler Pages. By then it was too late. The same elderly waiter with the immaculately starched white shirt and the knee-long navy-blue apron, fast as lightning in spite of his bow legs (you must remember him, the waiter we invited to dinner on board once?), had already served us the usual delicious roasted lamb with a bottle of Binisalem wine when, all of a sudden, Albert, looking quite flustered, fell silent. He took a maroon box out of his breast pocket, put it on the table and quickly said: "Katharina – I wonder whether you would grant me a wish?"

' "What is it?" I asked, hoping he couldn't hear my heart's wild pounding.

' "Please open this box," he said.

'I hesitated before picking it up.

'Of course I knew its contents.

'Werther, my husband – forgive me if you can – I desired it.

'And feared it.

'I took the ring out of the box and held it by the light of the candle.

' "It is not much – I know," Albert apologised hurriedly. "But it belonged to my mother. And to her mother before that."

'I was indeed relieved not to be holding the sort of huge, vulgar jewel that would only have made me feel cheap. This was a plain ring in yellow gold, discreetly ornamented with guilloche.

' "My God! Albert – why – thank you – please, please don't be upset . . . but you know I cannot accept it," I stammered.

' "Will you at least try it on?" he begged.

'Shaking my head, I indulged him. First, one after the other, I tried it on all the fingers of my right hand, but it did not fit. Then on the fingers of my left hand. I was acutely aware of his quick and shallow breathing as he leant forward, his face inches away from mine. The ring was too big for my little finger, too small for all the others – except my ring finger.

'On which I already wore a ring. The wedding ring that you, Werther, had firmly placed on it. I held my hands up to the flame of the candle, hoping its flicker would conceal the tears welling up in my eyes.

'"You see," I whispered. "It doesn't fit. I'm sorry, Albert."

'He grabbed my hand. "Will you let me try?" he asked.

'Before I could answer he gently tried to take my wedding ring off my finger. I was petrified – heavy-hearted at the pain I was inflicting on him. We were both surprised when the ring stopped before the first joint. When he gave it a sharp jolt, I let out a little squeal – more surprise than pain, really. He immediately stopped, put my hand to his mouth, lightly kissed my ring finger and released me.

'"I'm sorry," he said, with the saddest smile I've ever seen. "I didn't mean to hurt you. I should have known. Will you give me no hope whatsoever?"

'Looking into his eyes, I remained silent.

'"Unfortunately my love for you cannot be extinguished – not even by you," he whispered. "Katharina – I'll wait for you. Just – do not reject me. Please accept me – as your friend. I'll never pester you again. I promise. That was stupid. Bloody stupid."

'Tears were now running down my burning cheeks. He had to wait several minutes while I struggled to find a dry corner in my starched napkin, trying not to make a complete fool of myself. Out of the corner of my eye I could see our old friend the bow-legged waiter anxiously hovering quite close.

'"Don't say that!" I implored, taking his hands in mine. "You've done me the greatest honour. How can

I find words to thank you for your extraordinary kindness? Your generosity? Your . . . your love? I am not worthy of such love. Thank you, Albert. Thank you, thank you. I'll treasure this moment for the rest of my life. But – please understand . . . I am still a married woman."

'He closed his eyes, straightened his back and put his hands in his lap.

' "You yourself advised me to wait at least a year before seeking out my husband," I pleaded. "I cannot wait that long, but after Easter I shall go back to him. If he's back to his old self, I shall thank God, ask Werther to forgive me, and serve and honour him for the rest of my life. What else can I do?"

'I wiped my eyes again.

' "And . . . if he's not back to his old self?" he asked so quietly I could hardly hear him.

' "If Werther, my husband, has died – or turned into an alcoholic wreck – then I shall mourn him from the bottom of my heart, and ask God to forgive me for having failed him," I answered.

'Albert was staring into my eyes so intently that, in order to conceal my inner turmoil, I quickly stroked his cheek and got up.

'So it was, my very own love, that in the spring I returned to Portosirena to look for you.

'You'd gone.

'From our old landlady I understood I'd missed you by a few weeks at the most. But she couldn't give me any clue as to your whereabouts.

'I went through the empty house with a fine tooth-comb, and found no trace of you. Not even your smell.

'I asked my brother to ring your mother. He reported that she'd heard from you only once, soon after I had left. Apparently you'd been enquiring about me.

'I spent a week, roaming in the marina and the adjacent village, in Barcellona and Falcone, hoping that your old drinking mates might have some information. In vain. I tried the postman – but he had no forwarding address.

'And then I understood.

'The reason why you'd left no clue was that you did not want me to find you. You had cast me out of your life. Moved on.

'It was my fault. I had left you. Left you in your hour of need. So I understood your decision. I only needed to know that you were cured, that you had beaten alcoholism. Then somehow I would have resigned myself, possibly even been reasonably happy. I had to know what had become of you, and hear from you that you had repudiated me.

'For the last four years my life has been suspended. It will remain so until I find out whether I still am a married woman or not. Until I find you. Then, in Portosirena, I had no idea where to begin looking.

'At least, not until the day Roberto, that marine electrician mate of yours, came back from one of his many "holidays". Do you remember how he used to disappear for days on end after drinking himself into oblivion? Maybe you don't. When I saw that giant of a man, his face black with a week's stubble, loitering unsteadily on the pontoons, looking for work, I ran after him.

'Though he did not recognise me, his eyes lit up when I mentioned your name. It took me half an hour to explain to him that you'd disappeared and I was looking for you. First he shrugged his shoulders and threw up his hands – but I wouldn't let go. "Dove? Dove Werther?" I kept repeating. "Africa," he suddenly said. I thought I had misheard and summoned some of the tourists who had gathered around us to translate all my questions. "Africa," Roberto kept saying in an interrogative tone. That's all I could get out of him. He seemed to be under the impression that you had mentioned Africa, but could remember no more. Which part of Africa? What country? What for? Roberto didn't have the faintest idea.

'Of course, I was sure you would be doing something worthwhile out there, probably with some humanitarian organisation, maybe dealing with children. I assumed you'd be in places whose language you spoke, which ruled out French West Africa and those parts that speak Portuguese. Namibia and English-speaking Africa sounded like good bets. I decided to contact the embassies and all major aid organisations in those countries and, God willing, would soon trace you.

'Albert gave me the money to fly to Lagos and start my quest.

'For the first six or twelve months I remained hope-

ful. There were so many countries, so many embassies and consulates, so many NGOs and private charities! My postbag was enormous. And repetitive. Nobody had seen you, come across you, heard of you. In all those countries the expatriate community is quite small, and its German component minute; soon all of these communities knew about the German woman in Lagos looking for her husband all over Africa.

'Yet – no lead, no sighting, no clue ever turned up. Nothing.

'And so I now wonder whether Roberto invented this African story just to get rid of me – a mad German woman embarrassing him on the quayside at Porto-sirena, in front of his friends.

'After four years, I cannot believe that, if you really were in Africa, I wouldn't have come across you. My love – I now fear, I now feel that we are continents apart.

'Perhaps you are back home? Perhaps your mother knows your whereabouts? Perhaps you will eventually come back to her? She's my last hope.

'I have found work in a Lagos orphanage for another two years. If I do not hear from you during this time, it will be clear that you have either repudiated me, or disappeared from the face of the earth. Whichever is the case, this earth cannot be home for your wife.

'Werther – my beloved husband – my own and true and only and eternal love – be yourself. Be my light – as I used to be yours.

'Be strong.

'We shall be reunited.

'Your loving wife Katharina'

'So you knew where to find her?' I asked as soon as Kurt fell silent, hoping he wouldn't notice the tears silently running down Cathy's cheeks.

'Alas – I only discovered these letters some six years after they had been written – by which time Katharina had long left the Lagos orphanage. So I found myself in an identical quandary to hers, trying to locate her all over Africa, but with even more limited means. I had no money to travel, and, like her, had to contact all possible officials, organisations and charities. My quest was as unsuccessful as hers had been. The trail was not only cold: it had vanished.

'After six months in Hamburg, largely spent expediting my inheritance business, I was at a loose end. The Kurt who, in his mid-forties, had come back from ten years of war had nothing in common with the boy named Werther who'd grown up in this city. I had no family, no place of my own, and no desire to seek out those few acquaintances of old who might still be around. When people addressed me as Werther I tended to ignore them – not intentionally, but because I was Kurt. I was on my own, free-floating and insecure. My mother's death had deprived me of both women in my life: she'd been my only hope of finding the thread that might lead me to Katharina. Yes, after all these years, my whole being was still aspiring to one thing and one thing only: to be reunited with my wife. For Katharina was still my wife. Not only legally, since we'd never even discussed divorce, but also physically and spiritually. For some thirteen years I had not looked at another woman, let alone touched one – much to the bewilderment of my fellow Legionnaires, for whose gratification entire bordellos operated in the vicinity of our barracks. There had been nothing heroic, no abnegation or sacrifice involved in my reticence: I was in love with my wife. I guess it makes no sense to you?'

Cathy, who had listened to Katharina's letters almost in a trance, finally seemed to come back to life. Though shivering, instead of snuggling up to me on the cockpit bench she inched away from me again and, bringing her knees up, curled up almost into a foetal position.

'Why should it not make sense?' she murmured.

Not wishing to delay Kurt's narrative, I remained silent. If truth be told, I harboured some doubts about the possibility of remaining chaste for decades simply because one's wife has walked out on one. The man's libido had probably been suppressed by the onset of depression. I was also beginning to feel suspicious about the truth of this whole story. At any rate I couldn't see how my views were relevant. Thankfully Kurt did not wait for them before resuming:

'I never doubted that Katharina still loved me, and that as soon as we found each other she would realise that it was safe for her to come back to me. My remorse would be obvious, my enduring love plain to see, and she would quickly guess what hellish desert I had walked across in order to beg her forgiveness. If we were lucky, there might just be time for a couple of children; after all, she was younger than me. When I dreamt of her, which was most nights, she was even more ravishing in her maturity than she'd ever been in the glory of youth. But where on earth was she?

'It seemed that, since my chances of tracking Katharina down were non-existent, she would have to find me. As my mother's house had been sold, the only place she might expect to pick up my trail was where she'd left me: Portosirena. Besides, I needed to work. It was a wild card, but the only one in my hand. And so I decided to return to Portosirena and wait for my wife there. Of course I continued to correspond with all embassies and consulates and organisations I could think of. In case Katharina looked for me in Germany, I wrote a short note to Herr Doktor Miersch in Hamburg and to her brother in Berlin to inform them of my plan; then I packed my bags and left.

'Time had been unkind to Portosirena. The complex had aged prematurely. You've been there recently: you know what I mean. Ten years ago, the signs of decay were beginning to appear. The marina was only half full. The over-ambitious scheme to build several tranches of holiday villas within its fortifications had produced dozens of abandoned, half-finished building sites. Most of the sea-front shops were empty or shut. All the restaurants with their sonorous names – you probably remember them too, Sapori di Mare, Club Ulisse, La Cantina, and of course the Yachting Club – were shut most of the time, and almost as quiet and deserted during their rare opening hours. How they survived as commercial entities was a mystery; one heard rumours of money laundering and Mafia involvement. The dereliction of the buildings had been nature's good fortune. Acres of flowering purple bougainvillaeas covered the cracks on the walls, and the air was filled with the heavy scent of jasmine.'

'I remember!' Cathy cried. She has a passion for plants, and an encyclopaedic knowledge of them. 'And the giant geraniums? Did you see them?'

'Indeed; at the time, they were only beginning to win their competition with the oleanders. In fact they were fast expanding beyond the unkempt flower beds initially assigned to them. Cacti and maritime pines, feeble plants when I had left them, had grown majestic, colonising the red earth and blue skies. And what about the mimosas and gorse under the shade of the rubber trees – weren't they beautiful?'

'Yes! Did you smell the sage, the mallow and the fennel?' she retorted. 'God, how I loved those aromas of myrtle and rosemary and lavender! What a pity the sea never smells so good!'

'Cathy, please,' I groaned. 'How is Kurt supposed to get to those stinking corpses on his boat if you keep interrupting?'

'When I walked from the marina to my room in nearby Barcellona,' Kurt resumed, looking straight into Cathy's eyes, 'the orchards on both sides of the road seemed neglected, citrus lay rotting on the ground. In the ungroomed olive groves, myriads of yellow and mauve flowers, whose names I wouldn't know in German, let alone any other language, attested to the pointless beauty of a universe in which Katharina was missing. Never before had I come across such a gratuitous floral display; day after day, its abundance and brilliance astonished me. At first, I tried to learn some plant names, but soon decided such knowledge would in no way increase my enjoyment of them. After all, I was a simple German skipper, and whilst I knew a marlin from a swordfish and a bass from a bream, I am no expert on flowers. Suffice it to say that every day I collected a fresh bunch for my room, in readiness for Katharina's return.'

Suddenly Kurt fell silent. I wondered whether he was simply catching his breath, or perhaps had become aware of my fidgeting. Indeed my growing perplexity was rapidly turning into irritation. His story was turning into flowery ramblings, which did not bode well for our chances of getting some rest. Above all, he spoke too ornately. Admittedly, his mother was half English, and literate foreigners quite often speak English better than we natives; not only have they spent more time learning the rules, but they also feel more compunction about breaking them. Question of pride, I suppose: foreigners fear that any liberty they choose to take with our language could be misinterpreted as ignorance. Fair enough. Nevertheless, Kurt was no ordinary German – that much was clear. He was, in fact, anything but the 'simple German skipper' he pretended to be. Was he simply trying to impress us? To be honest, I found it disconcerting that the man should appear out of nowhere, and then proceed to tell my wife night-long stories in better English than I, an Oxbridge-trained native, could ever hope to muster. OK, there were the guttural sounds, the metallic accent, the odd intonations. Much more striking though was the fact that, while he sometimes seemed to be talking off the cuff, mostly he sounded as if he was . . . reciting. Yes: narrating a memorised tale. Was this his swan song? Surely, in his present condition, the altruistic desire to indulge Cathy's curiosity was less than overwhelming? Admittedly, he must have noticed how mesmerised she was – fascinated in fact. Perhaps he sensed what a sucker she is for a love story – any love story. Maybe he knew that, much to my dismay, she wouldn't let him go before getting some answers.

'Did you ever find your wife? Or did all those flowers go to waste?' she asked.

'I kept waiting. And hoping. And waiting. In order to earn my living, I started a diving and sailing school, relying mostly on British and German tourists. Of course that only kept me busy four or five months a year. The rest of the time, I reverted to boat supervision and maintenance. The third year I took a group of divers to Cuba for a diving holiday. I spent three weeks diving, fishing – and sleeping with every mulatta in sight.'

It wasn't without some satisfaction that I heard the sigh that deflated Cathy. It could do her no harm to realise that all men are fallible.

'There was no risk of emotional involvement,' Kurt continued without looking at her. 'It felt safe, and diminished my sense of infidelity. It probably kept me sane as well. I returned every year, but never touched a woman the rest of the time. I did not – do not – want anybody to stand between Katharina and me.'

'So you still haven't found her?' Cathy whispered. 'After all these years – you are still waiting?'

'Katharina hasn't returned yet. At the time she'd been missing for some fourteen years. Today it is closer to twenty-four. Am I still waiting? I might have been – until last week. But no more. What would be the point?'

I felt this sounded somewhat melodramatic, but kept my own counsel. Unfortunately Cathy did not.

'One should never give up waiting for the loved one,' she protested. 'Don't you agree, Terence?'

Before I could ask her to stop interrupting – since otherwise we stood no chance of getting to the end of the tale – Kurt had answered.

'There must be more to life than waiting,' he said gravely. 'Let me move on to the last chapter. Your husband is yawning, and soon it will be light.'

4

Suddenly the intermittent beeps of my watch alarm made us all jump. It felt like more than an hour had elapsed since I'd set it, but in the dark I couldn't see the time.

'I need to go and check on my daughter,' I said. 'Do carry on with your story: I'll be right back.'

'How is your hand?' Cathy asked Kurt.

For the last hour he'd been sitting in a slightly twisted position, his mangled hand in his lap. I was still wondering through which strange power of speech he'd kept us so enthralled in spite of his unnatural immobility and flat, guttural delivery. He didn't stir and ignored Cathy's question.

Cathy rose.

'You probably need a break,' she told him. 'I certainly do.'

While she made her way to the heads, I went down below and slowly opened Lucy's door. In the stifling darkness, I listened to her fast and shallow breathing.

'Lucy, my darling, are you asleep?' I whispered.

Her silence convinced me she was. I decided I should have a quick peek at her and turned on the reading light. When I turned round, Lucy was staring straight ahead with wide-open, blank eyes. I took her hand. It was burning.

'Lucy, baby, it's me,' I said softly. 'It's Daddy. How are you feeling, you poor thing?'

While her bandaged head remained immobile, her eyes slowly turned towards me but seemed to remain unfocused. Trying to get through to her, I kept repeating the same questions: 'How is your head, you poor darling? Does it hurt? Are you thirsty?'

Under my barrage of questions, she became more and more agitated, till an expression of sheer terror distorted her little face; in her confusion she kept muttering: 'Daddy – no! Please, Daddy? No – Daddy – please leave me alone!'

I heard Cathy on her way back from the heads. Just as I turned the light off, she came up behind me and peered into the cabin over my shoulder.

'How is she?' she asked.

'She's half asleep, possibly having some nightmare,' I said. 'But I managed to get her to drink some water.'

'Oh, well done,' Cathy said. 'That's progress. She doesn't feel feverish, does she?'

'Not in the least.'

I don't know why I lied.

Yes I do.

I lied because I saw no merit in Cathy witnessing the

delirious terror that I seemed to inspire in Lucy. What would have been the point?

I didn't budge, blocking Cathy's way, until she lifted the head she had rested on my shoulder to listen to Lucy's breathing and said: 'Resting and drinking are the best things for her. If you let me through, I might just check her pulse.'

'Don't bother. I've just done it. It's normal.'

Cathy hesitated for a couple of seconds.

'Have you reset your watch alarm?' she asked.

I fumbled with the tiny buttons in the dark.

'There,' I replied. 'One hour from now. You go back. I'll be right up.'

As soon as she disappeared I turned the light on again, filled a tumbler with water and tried to get Lucy to drink. It became immediately clear that her nightmare wasn't over; every time I touched her or tried to induce her to take a sip she seemed to become more frightened, and her moans were increasingly noisy.

'Lucy! Lucy, darling! It's me! It's your daddy!' I kept whispering. 'Don't be afraid, my darling! You know I'd never hurt you! But you must try and drink a little bit. Come on – just a few drops!'

She was getting hysterical.

'No! No! No! Daddy, please go away! Leave me alone!'

'It's all right, darling, it's all right,' I reassured her. 'It's all right. Just relax now. You can go back to sleep. You'll drink later. Don't worry. You calm down now. That's my girl.'

I switched the light off. That seemed to do the trick: Lucy soon stopped sobbing and her breathing regained some kind of regularity. It seemed that my intervention had done her more harm than good, and I reasoned that we might as well let her sleep for another hour, till dawn broke.

I was only halfway up the companionway leading to the cockpit when Kurt launched into the final chapter of his tale.

'Some five years ago, as I was hosing down the decks of one of my client's boat, a motor yacht slowly, hesitantly entered the marina. I was far too busy to pay any attention – till I realised, first, that she was attempting to moor in the adjacent space and, second, that the crew were out of their depth, and therefore likely to inflict damage on their neighbours. The French flag flying tautly across the top of the canopy above the aft deck showed the strength of the wind. The mooring arrangements in Portosirena are untypical of Mediterranean ports; with only centimetres to spare on either side, one has to reverse slowly into the narrow gap between two huge poles that emerge from the water and on which the lines securing the bow will be made fast, whilst attempting to secure the stern to the quay. Even with good visibility astern (which this boat did not offer), it is not the most practical system. With any crosswind, it demands the sort of boat-handling skills that the newly arrived crew clearly lacked. There were only two of them: an elderly man on the flying-bridge, and a not-so-young woman on the aft deck, boathook in hand. After the third or fourth attempt, they finally succeeded in squeezing their boat into the gap, not without acquiring a few dents on both sides of the hull. I stood ready to take their lines, for which they were grateful. That's how I became acquainted with *Gwelan II*.'

With his good hand, Kurt touched the gleaming hull of the sinister boat that blocked our horizon. I was glad he seemed to have finished explaining the mooring arrangements at Portosirena, since Cathy and I knew them well. I also knew by now that trying to interrupt him was futile; his story would unfold at his own rhythm, to the bitter end. At least he was now attacking the last five years of his saga.

'Believe me,' Kurt began again, 'this ship was no pretty sight. She was only some ten years old at the time, but the teak decks were warped, the stainless steel rusty, the hull pockmarked by innumerable dents and dirt from chafing fenders, and the engines emitted more black smoke than a Russian power station. That evening, her owners, Pierre and Yann Le Bihan, invited me on board for a drink. Pierre, a retired French paediatrician well into his seventies, is short, rotund and immensely jovial. Under a shock of snow-white hair and behind thick glasses, his blue eyes always sparkle as though meeting people were an ever-amusing privilege. Throughout nearly half a century of married life, Yann has loyally supported him as a nurse, practice manager, administrator, secretary and receptionist. She is only a couple of years younger than her husband, but much more agile. It is almost no exaggeration to say that, whereas Pierre is shaped like Bibendum, the Michelin man, and just about as cuddly, Yann is as thin as a stick and keeps herself very much in trim. Since they spoke no other language, they were much relieved to be able to converse with me in French. In reply to their compliments, I simply nodded, without mentioning that I had polished my French during ten years in the Legion. They never had children. Perhaps that explains why Pierre had not retired before seventy, since his profession allowed both of them to devote themselves to the children of others. They lived in Brest, and their passion was the sea. Over the years they had owned several sailing boats; then, in their sixties, they had switched to motor boating and moved to the Mediterranean. However, it soon became clear that *Gwelan II* was too much of a handful for them. They had bought her second-hand, perhaps without fully realising that these Taiwanese boats, cheap though they are, demand constant care and investment. Pierre was getting more and more arthritic, and they were clearly losing the maintenance battle.

'I mentioned that I was running a boat-maintenance business, and soon found myself working on various more or less urgent repairs on their behalf. It turned out that, in order to save money, they had left the South of France and decided to base themselves in Portosirena, at least for the coming season. One thing led to another; soon they asked whether I would be interested in working on *Gwelan II* as a live-aboard skipper. Although I hadn't captained a ship for years, I didn't hesitate long.

Of course they could pay me only a fraction of what I used to earn as a captain, and there would be no other crew; nevertheless, the lure of a steady income, however meagre, was irresistible. Living on board had two further advantages: I would save on rent, and feel much happier being on the water again. Besides, Pierre did not object to my keeping my other activities running; we shook hands on the deal. The arrangement worked well.

'Over the last few years I rejuvenated *Gwelan II*: stripped and reconditioned the engines, re-planked the forward deck and re-caulked the aft one, repaired the gelcoat wherever necessary and repainted the hull – you name it. Soon, when the sun rises, you will see that she is better than new – and this cost Pierre almost nothing.'

For half a minute, Kurt absent-mindedly stared at the bulky mass of glass-reinforced plastic that towered above us; then, like a free-diver preparing to plunge, he took a deep breath and resumed:

'I'm sorry. You are incredibly patient. Let me just briefly tell you about the last week of my life.

'Early last week I had an appointment with the marina shipyard to lift the boat out of the water for her annual pre-season cleaning, scrubbing and anti-fouling. *Gwelan II* is almost too big and heavy for the local facilities; she just fits in the lifting dock and her thirty tonnes test the local crane to its limit. In previous years, I had moved her under the crane all by myself without problems, but this time a strong *libeccio* was blowing, and I needed assistance with lines and fenders. The marina office promised to send me a *marinaio* for eight o'clock. Nobody had arrived by ten. I went to the office. They explained a mix-up had taken place; their insurance policy did not permit staff to work aboard clients' boats. Nothing would make them change their mind. This left me in the lurch; half the morning was gone, and if I lost my craning slot, at the busiest time of year, I might have to wait for weeks to get another one. As I walked back to the boat, wondering whether to risk going it alone despite the howling wind, I noticed two men having breakfast on the terrace of the waterfront café. On the spur of the moment I walked over to them. They turned out to be English. I apologised, explained I had been let down by the marina, and asked whether by any chance either of them might be willing to lend me a hand to move my motorboat to the crane, which should take under one hour. The tallest one, Paul, said he had to make a couple of telephone calls to order parts for his yacht, but would be with me within thirty minutes. I apologised again, explained to him where to find *Gwelan II* and returned to her in order to ready her for departure.

'Paul duly showed up and proved a most competent crew. After the boat was out of the water and safely chocked up on the hard, I gave him a lift back to his own sailing yacht, a magnificent Hallberg-Rassy. By way of thanks, I invited him and his friend Tom for a bite at one of the local restaurants that evening. At that point I wasn't quite sure which one owned the Hallberg-Rassy; it turned out that Paul did, and that Tom was a paid hand. Paul accepted the invitation, but mentioned that his niece and her husband had rented a flat in the marina complex and might also be around. It was too late to back off; furthermore I hadn't been close to a young woman for months, so I told him that the size of the party was no problem: the more, the merrier. Tom suggested I should first come to his boat for a drink around seven, then we'd all walk to the restaurant together.

'When I turned up that evening, their boat was a building site. Paul apologised, explaining that they had discovered unexpected problems, and were running late. He handed me a glass of water and invited me to sit down in the saloon till they tidied the place up. It was a mess. Whole floor panels had been lifted, revealing the miles of pipes and wiring that run all over a modern boat; dismantled pumps, voltmeters, electronic control panels, dozens of spanners, Allen keys and screwdrivers, tool-kits, electric drills, bits of piping and wiring almost blanketed out the glowing, rich-red mahogany. In order to sit down, I had to dislodge a hammer perilously perched atop a high pile of instruction manuals. It transpired that Tom was in the process of installing a whole new holding-tanks system. Now, as you no doubt realise, this is a major venture, which most owners would happily entrust to a specialist yard; but Tom and Paul were confident in their ability to do the work better and cheaper by themselves. By the time I had finished my glass they had cleared a few more square centimetres, sat down with flushed faces and opened two cans of Peroni. Paul explained that they were hoping to finish the work and sail away within a few days; I was sceptical, but said nothing. Suddenly, a tremor went through the boat, as somebody walked up the gangplank. A pair of immaculate white shoes, followed by white designer jeans, followed by a white designer polo shirt appeared on the companionway steps. "This is Akzo, my niece's husband," Paul said to me before turning to the young man. "And this is Kurt, who's generously offered to treat all of us to dinner tonight. By the way, where's Piggy?"

'I am not getting any younger, and the repeated firing of machine-guns and mortars has affected my hearing. I assumed, therefore, that I had misheard both names – easily done, particularly with foreign names. Yet, over the following days, I couldn't get a better fix on them. I am pretty sure that Akzo wasn't really called Akzo, but couldn't get behind the English pronunciation of whatever name might be his; as for Piggy, it soon became apparent why she could have borne no other.

'Akzo, a healthy-looking young man of medium height and build, in his mid- to late twenties, extended his right hand with a warm smile. He had a round, almost baby-like face and hair so blond you might have mistaken him for a Dane. "I feel happiness," he said.

' "Pleased to meet you too," I replied.

' "Piggy – she stands on pavement," he said in answer to Paul.

' "I am afraid my niece doesn't like boats very much," Paul explained to me. "In fact she has real problems moving about on them. Shall we go?"

'As we trooped off the boat I was curious about the young woman who preferred standing alone on a pontoon to sitting down in such a well-appointed craft as a Hallberg-Rassy 53. By that time she was actually sitting on the low wall that separated the quay from the gardens, surrounded by a cloud of tobacco smoke. I was so ill-prepared for what I saw that the shock of it stopped me in my tracks halfway up the gangplank; indeed I nearly lost my balance. Instantly I wished I could back out of the whole damn evening. "So you are the lonely skipper who can't move his boat by himself?" she croaked before her uncle could make the introduction. "Good looking, too!" The grating voice sent shivers down my spine. It was worse than a heavy-smoker's voice, rasping and shrill at the same time, throaty as well as nasal – above all, it was loud. Penetrating.

' "This is Piggy," her uncle said, bending low to kiss her cheek whilst we all formed a semi-circle in front of her. "Shall we walk to the restaurant, darling?" he asked. Helped by her husband, she got up with difficulty. "You can see why Piggy isn't too keen on negotiating our flimsy gangplank," Paul said to me. Indeed I could. Not because she was fat – fat people can be quite lithe. Nor obese – most obese people learn techniques to displace their bulk. No. This creature was beyond corpulence, beyond obesity: she was . . . gross. Her balloon-shaped body was clad in a formless pink blouse and flowery Bermuda shorts that ended where you would expect knees to be, revealing pink calves twice the diameter of a footballer's ham. Her arms, pushed away by bulbous flesh, left her shoulders almost horizontally. You could see that her breasts were gigantic, but there was no telling how they combined with her multiple chins or connected with the folds of her abdomen. I tried to avert my gaze, as one does when faced with a cripple, a beggar or a freak – but her little eyes held mine captive. They were no more than slits on top of the minuscule upturned nose that marked the centre of her puffed-up face – yet they kept me enthralled. I wasn't close enough to ascertain their colour; yet, as she ironically inspected me from top to bottom, stopping longer than necessary around my crotch, I felt their malevolence. The greasy, colourless hair that hung flatly down her temples gave no more clue to her age than the rest of her body. Taking into account the likely age of her uncle and husband, I deduced that, despite her worn appearance, she was unlikely to be more than forty, but I could easily have been out by ten years in either direction. Apparently, overweight people put so much strain on their knees that they eventually destroy them. As we made our way along the waterfront to La Cantina, though I wasn't sure whether she was heavily limping or simply tottering under her own weight, it became clear that Piggy could walk only slowly. In spite of our efforts to stroll along as leisurely as possible, Paul, Tom and I soon found ourselves well ahead of the couple. Tom explained to me that his niece had only been married for one year, and that Akzo was Albanian. His tone implied, in the nicest possible way, that this wedding had been a most pleasant surprise. I sat down at the end of a rectangular table, Paul on my left and Tom on my right; they ordered more Italian lagers, I a big bottle of San Pellegrino water. The absurd couple appeared some ten minutes later – the woman heavily leaning on the arm of her angelic husband. Her bulk was such that, although no taller than him, she not only dwarfed him completely, but lent him an innocent pageboy's look. As they inched their way to our table, the background volume of conversation dropped noticeably; of course, ten seconds later, it built up again: after all, this was Sicily. I rose as they approached. Neither Paul nor Tom moved.

' "Did you see this, dearest uncle?" she sneered. "That's what I call gentlemanly conduct. Totally misplaced, of course. Perhaps our lonely skipper thought I was a lady!" Painstakingly trying to lower herself into the chair opposite me, she guffawed loudly, echoed by my other guests. Akzo sat down next to her and unfolded a napkin on her bulging lap. When in position, the napkin floated horizontally a few centimetres higher than the table.

' "Would you like a drink?" I asked both of them. "I'm afraid we were too thirsty to wait."

'Akzo asked for a tomato juice, Piggy ordered two double whiskies. Nobody commented. During the course of the meal, I was grateful for the shield offered by both my neighbours. Given the Italian noise level, it was hard to talk across the table, and I was more than happy to talk boats with Paul and Tom. Out of the corner of my eye I could see that, though Piggy and her husband were actively engaged in conversation, she kept staring at me. Trying to keep my voice as low as practical, I asked Paul how his niece had come across her Albanian husband. To my surprise, he wasn't quite sure. "All I know is that she went to Albania a couple of years ago, stayed there for two months and came back with a husband," he said. When I pressed him a bit more, he confirmed that his niece neither spoke a word of Albanian, nor had any contacts in Albania before her trip; furthermore, at the time, Akzo did not understand a word of English. I expressed my admiration for the rapid linguistic progress the young man had made. "Very resourceful, these Albanians, you know," he said with a wink. I asked him what he meant. Before he could answer, Piggy's gravelly voice cut in. "Excuse me, lonely skipper – do you think we could have some more wine? It's getting a bit dry at our end of the table!" The three men were eating local grilled fish and sharing a bottle of Sicilian white wine; all by herself, Piggy had already drunk the bottle of red Chianti I had ordered to accompany her meat. In order to minimise her embarrassment, I asked for two more bottles, one of red and one of white. This was certainly going to be my most expensive evening in at least twenty years – though exactly how expensive only became clear a few days later. Piggy trained her piercing, bloodshot eyes on me. "Most generous of you, lonely skipper. Why are you drinking water? I thought all true mariners could hold their drink!" I muttered that I preferred water, but she made no effort to conceal her disbelief. I couldn't help feeling that, in the knowledge that many teetotallers are ex-alcoholics, she was seeking to humiliate me.

'Conversation resumed, and Paul undertook to educate me on Albania. Did you know that Albanians have a proud tradition of mountain banditry, well supported by a social system based on the blood laws of the clan, the *fara*? I learnt that, since their Stalinist regime imploded some ten years ago, organised government has virtually disappeared. It has been replaced by bands of gunmen running local fiefdoms and meting out their own brand of justice on the surrounding countryside. According to Paul, Albanian organised crime had grown so rapidly as to become a major threat to neighbouring countries such as Greece and Italy. I told him that, from my Sicilian vantage point, I had detected no trace of it: as far as one could see, it was pretty much business as usual for the Camorra.'

Kurt paused to catch his breath.

'But your friend Paul *was* right,' I interjected. 'Cathy – you remember my friend Mike Lively, the barrister?' She looked at me blankly. 'You *do* know him,' I insisted. 'We were at university together. Only last week he was telling me that soon a third of his clients would be Albanians – all paying top whack for top legal representation. He can't believe his luck. Apparently the Italian Mafia joined forces with the Albanians in lots of fields. Prostitution, money laundering, drugs trafficking: you name it. The bulk of all European heroin traffic now is in the hands of Albanians. They are taking over London like . . .'

'I believe you,' Kurt interrupted. 'The Albanians' truly distinctive talent is trafficking in humans. The so-called "Speedboat Mafia", specialised in moving contraband and people between Albania and Italy, is effectively running the official Albanian Government. They will never be short of clients, as Paul said with a wry smile. Nobody wants to live in such a shithole anyway. At least a third of the Albanian population had already crossed the EU border illegally, and, given half a chance, the remaining two-thirds would run too. "Fantastic business opportunity," Paul chuckled. "In fact the only growth industry in the region is the sex-slave trade. Poor gullible girls are either kidnapped or duped into coming to Britain with empty promises of a decent job. By the time they reach the UK, most of them have been forced to prostitute themselves, and so are putty in the hands of their new masters."

' "Who are these new masters?" asked Tom.

' "Oh, mostly enterprising Albanian men in their twenties, from the northern part of the country," Paul answered.

' "Is that where Akzo comes from?" I asked.

'Paul wasn't sure.

' "The only thing I know for sure is, you don't want to mess with them," he laughed. "They are extremely violent, and so far they're winning all the turf wars. Even against the Italian Mafia."

'I asked him why and how he knew so much about the Albanian Mafia. He replied that he had a curious mind and read the papers. By then it was getting late, and Piggy took advantage of the diminished background noise to join the conversation. She asked her uncle whether he'd been defaming Albania; Akzo was a patriot, she said, and he would be greatly saddened if this were the case. Looking at her adoringly, Akzo nodded enthusiastically.

' "My country, super country," he confirmed. "Only too poor. But I can get cheap Mercedes car for you."

'I must have looked surprised, so Paul explained that the Albanian gangs were so sophisticated that I could even specify the type, colour and options for my new Mercedes, which would be spirited away from Western Europe and available to me within weeks for a fraction of the usual price. "Of course," he added, "I wouldn't advise you ever to try and drive your Mercedes outside Albania; you may find it is quite quickly taken away from you!" I wasn't sure whether he meant the police would soon impound the car, or that more Albanians would steal it again, but joined in the general laughter. Then Piggy put her cigarette down, picked up her mobile phone and loudly announced she needed to check on her dad. "Hello, Dad, it's me," she bellowed into the mouth-piece. "Have I caught you at the wrong time? Were you just about to screw one of your ridiculous chicks?" She was talking too loudly for the rest of us even to pretend that we weren't listening, so we just waited. "No, we're still in Portosirena," she answered. "In fact we are in the middle of dinner – courtesy of a gorgeous-looking local skipper . . . Yes, of course he's here . . . How is the weather at home? . . . Why don't you leave your silly little tarts in London and come down for a few days? The weather is amazing down here."

'Now, I know the world is changing fast, but I was deeply shocked by the way in which this woman was talking to her father. Even in private, it would have been utterly disrespectful; in public, in front of complete strangers, it was offensive. Loathsome. Incredibly, the indulgent smiles still lingering on the faces of Paul, Tom and Akzo betrayed neither embarrassment nor disapproval; it was the slightly blasé expression of spectators who have perhaps seen the show too often.

'"Well, Dad, I shouldn't keep you away from your pussies for too long, should I?" Piggy was squeaking. "We wouldn't want them to dry up, would we? . . . I wish you'd stop fucking around like this, though – at your age, it can't be good for your heart! . . . Love you too."

'She hung up, put the phone down and announced that regrettably her father had declined her invitation. Looking me in the eyes, she explained across the table that her father had lately developed an appetite for very young women. Those diners still left at the neighbouring tables went quiet. In the sudden stillness, she recounted how, on a recent occasion, she had entered her father's home to find two stark-naked foreign girls in his bed, the combined age of whom, she stressed, did not add up to her own.

'"Don't you find it disgusting that men should shag girls half their daughter's age?" she asked me directly. All I wanted was for this meal to end promptly, so I nodded vigorously. Akzo roared with laughter and kissed her hand. "Of course, I am not saying that both partners should be *exactly* the same age," she smirked, tenderly patting the back of her husband's wrist. "Certainly not. Life wouldn't be worth living, would it, darling? But there should be limits – even for lecherous old men, don't you think, skipper?"

'I signed my credit-card slip, folded my napkin and got up without answering.

'That evening, having wasted some ten per cent of the meagre monthly salary that Pierre Le Bihan could hardly afford paying me, I returned to *Gwelan II* in a foul mood. I solemnly resolved to be more prudent in the future, and either to shun total strangers or accept invitations to nothing more than casual drinks. Having eaten more than usual, I was repeatedly woken during the night by oppressive nightmares in which all the monsters of my past seemed to have coalesced into one single ogress.

'Eager to expel Piggy from my head, I got up at dawn, and spent several hours polishing *Gwelan II*'s super-structure. I always take pleasure in this outdoors, physical work, not only because it numbs the mind, but also because I enjoy the transformation of matt, yellowish gelcoat to a glossy mirror. Pierre Le Bihan once told me that boats are like women: with the right amount of make-up, they can conceal their age almost indefinitely. By eleven o'clock it was getting hot – and I was getting thirsty. I decided to take my morning break, which usually involved sitting down at the waterfront café and catching up with last week's Sicilian newspapers. I ordered a large glass of water and one of those Italian espressos that, though they never amount to one whole mouthful, seem to linger on your palate for hours. The weather was as good as it gets in these parts – decorative filaments of strato-cirrus high up in the otherwise clear blue skies, a refreshing sea breeze building up as we approached midday. But perhaps you were already in Portosirena by then?'

'No,' I replied. 'We only arrived . . .' I stopped, surprised to find that I could not remember exactly when we'd arrived in Portosirena. My sense of time seemed to have become blurred. 'Now – Cathy, when exactly did we get to that marina?' I asked.

'About one week ago, I think,' she answered. 'I wonder why we didn't see Kurt or his boat at the time.'

'Of course, my boat was still out of the water, in the yard,' Kurt resumed. 'I would have remembered your Bowman if I'd seen her, we don't get many of those in Sicily. Anyway, my quiet enjoyment of the morning sun did not last long. Having positioned myself so that my head would be in the shade of a parasol, but my legs exposed to the rays, I was so absorbed in my reading that I only gradually became aware of an odd occurrence: my legs were getting cold. Indeed, they were now in the shade too. It was as though the sun's orbit had suddenly changed, or the parasol behind me surreptitiously moved. You know how it is with mariners: even on dry land, we unconsciously continue to pay attention to wind, clouds and planets. Without even looking up from my newspaper, I could see that the parasol's shade still was the same oval shape; only it seemed to have grown *bigger*. I was still pondering whether to move my chair half a metre to the right in order to get my legs back in the sun when a trumpet pierced my eardrums: "Good morning, lonely skipper! Mind if I join you?" Startled, I jumped up. There she was, grinning. The trumpet in my eardrums had been replaced by the pounding of my heart. I was trapped. I waved vaguely at the empty seat next to me. She struggled to get her midriff down into it, putting such strain on its plastic legs that they instantly started warping. From the terrified waiter – a young Italian, probably some student, who seemed to know her – she ordered a mix of *suppa inglese* and *ciocolatta* from the *gelati* stand, accompanied by a large cappuccino and croissant. I asked her whether she normally breakfasted in this café. Oh no, she answered, she'd already had breakfast in her rented flat; these were elevenses. "Akzo and I had a busy morning," she said with a wink. "Activity always seems to make me hungry." For the next ten minutes, I shifted on my seat, trying to steer the conversation towards neutral topics. Did she like boats? No, she hated all useless boys' toys. Did she like the seaside? Only the nudists' beach. What did she do in London? She helped her father run his business. What sort of business? A kind of lettings agency. What does that mean? In our case, it means letting the same rooms to dozens of stupid immigrants, she chuckled. What kind of immigrants? There is only one kind, she snarled, her mouth smeared with melting ice cream. But – enough about me. What about you, lonely skipper? You look like somebody who hasn't had a decent screw for yonks – right or wrong? Such a shame really. A great-looking fellow like you could bed any woman he wanted, surely? But perhaps you are into under-age sluts too, like my dad? What is it with you fucking old men – are you too fucking stupid to recognise a real woman when you see one?

'The urge to leave became so strong that I almost felt it as a physical discomfort. Unfortunately, the waiter had disappeared inside, probably watching football on the television set stuck up on the wall in the far corner. Rather than wait for the bill, I started fumbling in my pockets, trying to rustle up just enough to pay for our food and drinks without having to wait for change.

'"What's the rush, lonely skipper?" she asked, her voice fat with irony. "Are you so afraid of real women? Believe me, I'm not about to rape you. I won't even be able to get up from this chair without your help."

'She burst into laughter. She knew she'd just quashed my escape plan. The prospect of any physical contact with this freakish predator made my hair stand on end – but it was true that she'd never be able to get up on her own. What was I to do? For lack of a better idea, I asked what had brought her down to Portosirena, since she seemed fond neither of the sea nor of sailing. Not only did Akzo like boats very much, she answered, but he was also an experienced speedboat driver. Furthermore, Fikret, Akzo's younger brother, was getting married at the beginning of the following week – one year to the day after her own wedding. Her uncle had offered to take them both to Albania on his yacht for the combined wedding and anniversary, together with their cargo of presents for the whole family. What sort of wedding presents? I asked. Oh, the sort of silly hardware that all Albanians seem to like, she replied. I wondered how she fancied the thought of a crossing that, depending on the wind, might take a few days. Not one bit, she said: in fact she was now planning to let Akzo go on the bloody sailing boat and travel herself by regular ferry. What about flying? I suggested. Don't be ridiculous! Do I look the flying type? Even if there were a direct flight, they wouldn't have me. Besides, I don't think that engines powerful enough to lift a real woman like me into the heavens have been invented – unless German hydraulics are up to the job, lonely skipper? Kurt, I said. My name is Kurt. Is it really? she asked with a penetrating glance. A manly name, lonely skipper. Very manly indeed. I could not think of a better one myself.

'Just as I was looking at my watch for the third time – I had work to do – Akzo appeared on the waterfront. He came to us, waving cheerily, clad in a white short-sleeved cotton shirt, white jeans and the same white shoes he'd been wearing the previous night. His flaxen hair, swept back and probably held in place by some gel, reflected the sun like some kind of halo that, added to his cherubic smile, made him look like a first communicant. He bent down, tenderly kissed his wife on the lips and moved behind her chair, where he started to massage her shoulders.

'"How are you, Mr Kurt?" he asked. "Very much thanks for grand dinner last night. Very much good."

I nodded and got up, offering my seat to him, but it turned out that he had no time to stop. In fact, he had only come to inform his wife of an unfortunate development: working in the bilges of his boat, her uncle Paul had so contorted himself that he'd hurt his back, and now was in too much pain to move. When Piggy asked what this meant in terms of the planned cruise to Albania, Akzo could only shrug. I seized this opportunity to take my leave. As my way back to the yard took me past the Hallberg-Rassy, I decided to call in briefly and check whether Paul needed any help. I was greeted by Tom, who seemed to have exchanged his tools for a mug of white instant coffee. The boat was in the same chaotic state as on my previous visit, though yet more floor panels had been lifted, through which long wooden boxes were visible. This slightly surprised me, since I expected to see these spaces filled by plastic tanks, but all boats are different. I was taken to the master cabin where Paul was lying on the double bunk, his back supported by a sheet of plywood. It transpired that he had a history of back problems, and that such crises normally lasted anything between three days and two weeks. It couldn't have come at a more inconvenient time, he said, since he was committed to sailing to Albania within days – otherwise Akzo would miss his brother's wedding. I mentioned that Piggy had explained the plan to me, and that they probably should think about changing it, since neither craft nor crew looked likely to be operational in time. He agreed. I asked him whether I could be of any help – I spoke some Italian and knew the local doctor. He thanked me for my kindness and looked at me for a while. "Actually, there is one thing you might be able to do," he reflected aloud. "Have you ever chartered your boat?" I replied that the boat wasn't mine, but that the French owner was always looking for extra income to defray his costs. I also explained that

Portosirena was in no way an ideal chartering base, so that, much to the owner's chagrin, we couldn't expect more than a couple of clients a year, mostly for short trips.

' "I'll tell you what," Paul said excitedly. "Why don't we charter your boat for a few days? I guess that, without pushing your big engines, you could get from here to Durres in two days – couldn't you?" I confirmed that this sounded about right – weather permitting. Paul asked when *Gwelan II* might be craned back into the water, and got even more excited when I told him that, although I hadn't quite finished all the planned works on the superstructure, the hull would probably be clean, anti-fouled and seaworthy the following day. "Brilliant!" he exclaimed. "Then you should be ready to sail the day after tomorrow, which will give you plenty of time to arrive before the wedding." I asked who my passengers were likely to be. Akzo would probably be more than enough crew for such a short trip, he suggested, parti-cularly bearing in mind that he knew his home waters well; but Tom would be more than willing to help if I felt it necessary. I looked at Tom, whose nodding eloquently conveyed a clear message: anything to get away from the bilges of this boat! On the other hand, Paul continued, keeping Tom with him as a nurse, given his present predicament, wasn't without attraction – let alone the fact that work on the Hallberg-Rassy needed to continue. His head down, Tom now looked disappointed.

'Only because I owed Paul a favour, I told him that I would call the owner, and seek his instructions. When I finally got hold of Pierre Le Bihan later that evening, he was enthusiastic. In fact, he and his wife had been wondering how much longer they could afford maintaining such a big boat just for the two of them; any additional chartering income would certainly help to defer any painful decision for at least one more season. I pointed out that Albania was outside the cruising range permitted by our insurance policy, but he thought he could get it added for a nominal premium. I also reminded him that Albania was supposed to be the crime centre of the world, but he laughed my fears off. "What is it with you, Kurt?" he asked. "What happened to your sense of adventure? I only wish I could make the trip with you. What are you worried about? It's only a couple of days' sailing, and you don't even have to refuel there, do you?" I said that would largely depend on the weather conditions. "Anyway, you'll have an Albanian on board," he joked. "You'll be under protection!" I asked him how much I should charge for the charter. "As much as possible," he answered. "You know our costs as well as I do. If you could get ten thousand dollars plus our fuel costs, that would certainly take the pressure off." I told Pierre I would try my best and went back to the Hallberg-Rassy. Paul seemed slightly less uncomfortable, but he was still lying on his plank, unable even to lift his head without wincing. I told him that I had authority to charter *Gwelan II* for twenty thousand dollars plus fuel plus all incidental expenses, provided the return trip to Durres took less than a week. I expected him to be horrified; yet, to my dismay, he seemed relieved and thanked me for my intercession. I added that payment would, of course, have to be made in advance – which meant almost instantly, if we aimed at casting off within a couple of days. He didn't blink. "Of course," he repeated.

'By lunchtime the following day – that was only three days ago! – *Gwelan II* had been craned back into the water. Before driving her back to her mooring place, I topped up both fuel tanks in the hope that she might carry enough for the round trip. I spent the rest of the day provisioning and filled both fridges with enough victuals to last us a week. As you know, stocking up with drinks always requires the hardest work; however, the huge trolley available at the marina supermarket meant that a couple of return trips sufficed to bring on board the many bottles of mineral water and hundreds of cans of Peroni and Coke that would sustain Akzo and me.

'In the afternoon Tom and Akzo appeared, pushing and pulling heavily laden carts. By the time they had manoeuvred six long wooden crates up the quaking gangplank and deposited them on the aft deck, they were out of breath and sweating profusely. It turned out that these crates, similar to those I had fleetingly observed under their saloon floor, contained the presents for Akzo's brother and his family. It seemed pointless to ask questions, though I later established that each crate weighed the best part of fifty kilos. Tom and Akzo downed a couple of lukewarm cans of beer in quick succession. I asked Tom whether he carried any detailed charts of the Albanian coast aboard the Hallberg-Rassy, since mine were to the wrong scale and out of date. He replied he would have Akzo bring me his charts, and I agreed with Akzo that we would leave the following morning as soon as I had received the weather forecast. He smiled enthusiastically.

'The following morning at nine – that was the day before yesterday, I guess – except it is now well past midnight, so maybe it was three days ago – Akzo duly turned up, carrying two huge holdall bags. I assumed that his wife, who was standing next to him, had come to wave him goodbye. I was mistaken. She had decided to sail with us. "Lovely morning, skipper!" she called. "I thought I'd better keep an eye on you boys. It's not often that one gets the opportunity to travel on such a nice big motorboat!" I was . . . speechless. Laughing, Akzo climbed up the gangplank, dropped his two bags on the kedge locker and went down again, extending a muscular arm towards his wife. Slowly and perilously, grabbing Akzo's wrist with her right hand and the extremity of the overhead port davit with the other, she inched her way up. I watched in fascination, as one might watch the lethal dance of a cobra, all the time willing her to fall from the creaking aluminium gangplank to the bottom of the marina. No such luck: panting and grunting, she was on board. "Are you happy to see me, Mr Kurt?" she asked as soon as she got her breath back. "Much more fun having a woman on board, isn't it?" She guffawed noisily; Akzo dutifully echoed her. "By the way, I have a little present for you," she added. She fumbled in the pocket of her Bermuda shorts and handed me an envelope. Holding it by the tips of my fingers, I put it on the aft-deck table. "I think you'd better have a look," she insisted. "Ten thousand dollars in cash. Uncle Paul says the balance will be wired to your boss's account tomorrow." I saw a ray of hope. "But we'd agreed that full payment should be made in advance!" I protested, desperate to find them in breach of contract. To start with, I had certainly never agreed to carry this creature on my boat – be it for love or money. "You have nothing to worry about, lonely skipper," she reassured me mockingly. "You can ring your owner tomorrow; we'll still be within range. If he hasn't received the balance of the money, you can dump us overboard." Akzo burst into renewed laughter. "Besides," she went on, "perhaps your owner doesn't expect more than ten thousand dollars anyway? Then what would happen to this cash?" "Ten thousands dollar much cash in Albania," Akzo gravely confirmed. "Mr Kurt he buy my village for five thousand dollars." "Mr Kurt may only want to buy your women," she giggled. I was utterly confused. Had they simply guessed that I had doubled Pierre Le Bihan's asking price? And did they really assume that I had intended to steal half the proceeds from him? Perhaps they had been in touch with Pierre – I had given them his details so they could wire the money to him. I hadn't yet had a chance to report to Pierre the improved terms I had negotiated on his behalf; perhaps they believed they could blackmail me?

'For a couple of seconds the temptation to throw the money back at them and order them off my boat was almost irresistible. Only the thought of the disappointment this would cause Pierre and Yann stopped me. Despite my misgivings, I showed the couple into the owner's cabin aft and went to collect the weather forecast from the marina office. The confirmation that the prevailing anti-cyclonic conditions would guarantee superb weather for the foreseeable future held all the promise of a death warrant.

'Devoid of any excuses, I came back on board and forlornly conducted my engine checks. Both raw-water strainers were clear, the oil level in both engines was perfect, as was that in the gearboxes. I opened both engine raw-water stopcocks and checked for leaks: there were none. My only hope was some kind of battery problem or electrical fault that would prevent the engines from starting: I had hardly turned the key when they both sprang into life. Engine and gearbox oil-pressure gauges both in the green. Both alternators charging. *Verdammt!* I went to the aft deck to check on the exhaust water flow and smoke colour: everything perfect.

'I had to go.

'Starting from the bows and methodically moving aft, I gave my passengers the usual safety briefing. First, I distributed automatic life jackets and showed them how to inflate and adjust them. In Piggy's case this was a challenge, since none of the straps was quite long enough. In particular, the crotch one, supposed to prevent a casualty from sliding downwards through her life jacket and losing it over her head, was far too short. I guess I could have found some way of solving the problem, but, warned off by her lewd jokes, thought better of it. No way was I going to fumble around her crotch. I showed them the first-aid kit under the double bunk in the forward cabin, and how to operate both fire extinguishers and the fire blanket. I went through the procedure for MAYDAY distress signals on the VHF radio, making clear that only the skipper – assuming he was operational – was empowered to authorise such a call. I pointed to my box of distress flares, and briefly explained their use. I had them practise pumping the bilges manually, in case we developed a leak or shipped too much water for our three automatic bilge pumps to deal with. Then we moved on to the aft deck, and went through the "man overboard" procedure: throw a life ring, shout "Man overboard!", keep your eyes fixed on the casualty and point at him at all times. I demonstrated the launching of our eight-person liferaft, listed its contents, and explained that abandoning ship was very much a last resort. I asked whether they had any questions. They didn't.

'I had to go.

'I explained to Akzo the casting-off manoeuvre, slipped all but the last three lines and took control from the flying-bridge. On my signal, Akzo slipped the remaining lines in the correct order and coiled them quite professionally. He then went round the boat, collected all the fenders and put them away in their stainless-steel holders on the stern. The man knew what he was doing. Ticking along on one engine at some three knots down its glassy river mouth, we were out of the marina by ten. In spite of my detestable cargo, I was elated to hit the open sea, where the gentle thermal breeze raised only the daintiest of wavelets. We rounded Capo di Milazzo in flat calm conditions, the air still heavy with the earthy scent of pine trees, jasmine and wood fires. After several months confined in port, it is always a great delight suddenly to have one's horizon widen to infinity; such a release to smell that first whiff of undiluted iodine, the primal scent of the deep. Soon we left the Aeolian Islands and their terrible memories on our port quarter. Making good progress towards the Stretto di Messina, I spent the rest of the morning steering from the flying-bridge, secure in the knowledge that the short ladder leading up to it would guarantee its Piggy-free status more effectively than any edict of mine. I might have lost the enjoyment of the rest of my ship, but at least I could rely on this sanctuary.

'Every now and then, Akzo popped his head up and volunteered to relieve me or help in any way. I explained my watch plan to him: I was happy to be on duty all morning, then he could come on until nightfall, so that I might get some rest before attacking the night. He was agreeable to the plan and kept bringing me glasses of iced tea with lemon. In the early afternoon I came down to the saloon and asked him to keep a lookout for a while so that I could rustle up some lunch. Using some of the hard-boiled eggs I had cooked before our departure, I threw together a big salad, doubling the quantities I deemed necessary for just two men, put ten slices of ham on a plate together with German gherkins and butter and cut some bread. Akzo went to fetch Piggy, who was resting in the aft cabin, and both of them sat down for lunch at the saloon table, whilst I took my plate to the saloon helm seat in order to relieve Akzo. But first I had to crank the saloon table right up to the top of its stainless-steel leg, in order to allow Piggy under it. She was now jammed between seat and table, somehow spread out horizontally. Thus wedged and distorted, she seemed broader than ever.

' "Well, Akzo," I said, "you seem to know what you are doing on a boat, don't you? Will you be ready for the afternoon watch?" "Always ready," he laughed. "But not good with navigation." I explained to him that the ship's autopilot would be engaged, so that his task would solely consist of keeping a good lookout for traffic, and calling me if any shipping appeared within a radius of three or four nautical miles. He nodded. I complimented him on his skills as a deck hand and asked where he'd acquired them.

'Her mouth stuffed full of ham, Piggy interrupted me to praise her husband. He was a very clever man, she explained, skilled in the most diverse fields, and a man of honour too – a pity he'd had to leave Albania, since otherwise he would doubtless have risen fast and might even be a minister by now. I asked why Akzo had left his country. Akzo comes from a poor family in the north of Albania, she explained. When he was a child, both his parents were killed in a bus accident. Akzo, together with his younger brother and sister, Fikret and Adzovic, went to live with a maternal uncle. By the time Akzo was sixteen, he was away from home most of the time, employed by his uncle to make international deliveries. Returning after two months from one of these trips, he found that his sister, a pretty twelve-year-old schoolgirl, had disappeared. Complaining bitterly about the ingratitude of the girl, the uncle explained that she'd run away, and that all searches had been fruitless. However, there was nothing in Adzovic's character that might have given credence to such a story; she was a timorous child, still untroubled by the pangs of puberty and with hardly any friends apart from her two brothers. Akzo's suspicions were confirmed when Fikret told him that their uncle had spent hours smoking and drinking with two strangers the day before Adzovic had vanished. Soon Akzo understood that their uncle, in time-honoured fashion, had sold his niece to gangsters. Indeed he followed her trace up to Croatia, where she had been put to work as a child prostitute in an Adriatic resort, and then lost her. Apparently she had been smuggled into England, and there the trail went cold.

'Albanians have an ancient code of honour based on revenge, called *kanun*, so that Akzo had no choice: he had to kill his uncle, and duly did so. Of course the blood law of the clan, the *fara*, had then come into play, and Akzo's life had been in danger ever since. I asked him how it felt.

'"Never afraid," he replied with a shrug, pointing at his waist. He then lifted his loose-fitting white shirt to reveal a gleam of black steel on his left hip. It happened too quickly for me to identify the type of gun, but it certainly was no toy. Why was he now returning to Albania, I asked? He smiled and moved closer to me. "One, my brother wedding. Two, nobody expect me to arrive on French motor yacht. Three, once my family get wedding presents, all of us are safe for ever. You see?" I saw. There was probably enough hardware in these crates for a whole tribe to fight years of guerrilla war. I looked at him, wondering whether this was his idea of a joke, but he held my gaze with innocent round eyes, a blond, smiling child expectantly begging for approval. I dropped my plate on the table and went back to the wheel to ponder the implications of this revelation.

' "Now you know what my Akzo is made of, lonely skipper!" Piggy roared with laughter. "He's even shown you his gun – you lucky man! I bet you'd like to see Akzo's gun in action, wouldn't you? Akzo, darling, do you think we should organise some light entertainment for our skipper?" He was gazing at her with his beatific smile, the very picture of silent worship. "Well, perhaps a bit later," she concluded, rolling two slices of ham into a compact cylinder that she then stuffed into her mouth. "But only on a pay-or-play basis, skipper. Only pay-or-play." She had already drunk three cans of beer.

'As soon as lunch was over I retreated to the safety of the flying-bridge, leaving Akzo to clear up the table and do the washing up. After a while he climbed up the ladder to the bridge, carrying a tray laden with a cup of coffee, sugar, milk and a chocolate bar, his balance so perfect that even the bow wave of the Italian coaster which rocked us at that very moment failed to destabilise him. I was impressed to see that, instead of opting for instant coffee, he'd made use of our small espresso machine, which relies on being heated on the gas stove. It had been a long time since I had been so well treated by my crew. I asked him how to say thank you in Albanian and he told me.'

Kurt stopped for a while, his brow deeply furrowed.

'Believe it or not,' he resumed, shaking his head, 'I'm afraid I have already forgotten. Not that it matters in the least. I don't think I'll need it ever again. Anyway, we were making good progress, the sea so silky that I opened up the big Caterpillars to take full advantage of the conditions. You see, *Gwelan II* is a heavy boat, with an inefficient hull; with any head seas, as her bow ploughs in and throws up tonnes of water, she has a wet ride and consumes more fuel. It made good sense therefore to increase speed in those ideal conditions, where the oily water seemed to offer no resistance. My only concern was the extreme heat. The temperature in our engine-room was close to fifty degrees centigrade. As you know, hot air is less dense than cold air, and I was afraid that our big turbo-charged diesel engines might be getting less air than they needed. I put the engine-room ventilation fans to work and regularly checked our exhaust smoke, which seemed no blacker than usual.

'As we attacked the hundred-mile crossing of the Gulf of Otranto, there wasn't a boat to be seen on the horizon. I selected my radar's maximum range, which is twenty-four nautical miles, satisfied myself that there was no shipping ahead of us, got up, showed Akzo the skipper's seat and lay down on the port bench, my cap over my eyes. I didn't want to go down below: first, it was too hot inside; second, I wanted to stay well clear of Piggy. I spent the rest of the afternoon alternating between short and shallow naps, plotting our position on the map, ensuring that Akzo wasn't dozing off, checking the engines' oil pressure and temperature and making quick and frequent raids to fetch liquid from the fridges. On none of these forays did I see Piggy; I assumed that she had retreated to the aft cabin. Around six o'clock, Akzo asked me to take over whilst he went to relieve himself and check on his wife; he was back at the helm within ten minutes, having delivered more cans of chilled lager to the aft cabin and restocked the fridge with beer, water and iced tea. In preparation for a long night, I forced myself to doze. How interminable the hours of darkness would turn out to be, I couldn't possibly fathom; but every fibre of my being was longing for the instant when, both my passengers in bed, my ship would be returned for me to steer under the stars.

'We rounded Santa Maria di Leuca as the light was beginning to fade, but before the lighthouse lit up. An hour later I decided to go down before it was completely dark to prepare some kind of evening meal. As soon as night fell, I reduced our speed to nine knots, turned our running and dashboard lights on, dimmed the brilliance on the chart plotter and radar screens and called my passengers to dinner. I told them that we had to keep the saloon in semi-darkness in order to preserve my night vision. In reply to her question, I explained to Piggy that, after exposure to strong light, the human eye needs some ten to fifteen minutes to readjust to night conditions. She replied that this sounded like typical skipper's bullshit. I pointed out that it was a well-known fact that she could easily experience herself, here and now. But Piggy wasn't in a good mood. She was breathing heavily, almost winded by the effort of climbing the five steps that separate the galley from the saloon, and dripping with sweat. Her decision to spend the day in the aft cabin had been ill-advised; because both exhaust pipes run through it, it tends to get extremely hot – that day it must have been well over forty degrees centigrade in there. Her predilection for cold lager had left her much the worse for wear, her baleful face grey and the slits of her little eyes tighter than ever. "Nonsense," she insisted. "We haven't paid twenty thousand dollars to eat crap food in the dark, Mr Kurt – have we, my darling?" "Tomorrow, me buys six new S-class Mercedes for twenty thousands dollar," Akzo confirmed. 'Each Mercedes with very excellent light." They both burst into laughter as though sharing the best joke ever. "You see?" Piggy asked me. "All skippers are full of bullshit. Always trying to throw their weight about." I was surprised by her choice of expression, but restricted myself to filling our three plates with smoked salmon and taking mine back to the helm seat. "You're not listening, are you?" she barked. I replied I was. "Then I am going to tell you a story, Mr Flying Dutchman, or whatever you are," she retorted. "You think I am a revolting freak, don't you?" I did not like her rising excitement and protested meekly, trying not to antagonise her any further. I looked at Akzo: having squeezed half a lemon on top of his smoked salmon, he was buttering a slice of rye bread.

' "Don't you?" she repeated. "Of course you do. Look at me! Do you really think I was born like this? Well – I bloody well wasn't. I was the most adorable little girl you've ever set eyes on – my Akzo has seen the pictures, haven't you, my love?" His mouth full of smoked salmon, Akzo nodded. "I only became Piggy because of one of your kind," she continued, waving a flabby forefinger at me. I froze. Fortunately, I was standing in the dark behind the wheel, and she could not see my face. "When I was a child," she went on, "my parents had a motor yacht that was captained by a professional German skipper. The yacht was used for corporate entertainment, and my parents had to spend a lot of time with their guests, so that I was frequently left in the care of this skipper. However, unbeknownst to my poor parents, this man was the worst kind of pervert, a child molester who had no qualms whatsoever about exploiting the situation. I was not even six at the time. One day, the bastard decided to anchor in a ridiculously unsafe place – as it happens, we sailed almost past it this morning, it was in the Aeolian Islands. I nearly drowned in Lipari; in fact, had it not been for my parents' decisiveness in flying me out of there, I probably would have died. However, to make things worse, the German brute, in his clumsy attempt to rescue me, had damaged my ribs, lungs and spine. For several days, I remained in a kind of coma from which I emerged almost amnesic. It took me several months to learn to walk again, and I have limped ever since. There you have it, you fucking arrogant lonely skipper. Not a pretty story, is it? So, if you think I will take any bullshit from you, you'd better think again. Understand?'

'Afraid that she might detect my trembling, I firmly held on with both hands to the big wheel in front of me. She was staring at me, radiating pure hatred. "How do you know the story to be true?" I whispered. She dropped the plastic tumbler full of lager that she had just lifted from the table and stared at me uncomprehendingly, whilst Akzo calmly mopped up the spilt beer with all the paper napkins he could find. "What the fuck do you mean?" she grunted. Attempting a normal conversational tone, I repeated: "I mean, since you were very small, and amnesic after the accident, how do you know that the stories about the skipper are true?" "Oh, I see," she chortled. "You think I am making it up, don't you? Akzo, my darling, we thought our lonely skipper was a gentleman – and now he's saying to my face that he doesn't believe me – did you hear?" Akzo nodded gravely. "I hear clear and loud," he confirmed. "Mr Kurt he's making error." "All I meant was that somebody must have told you the story," I interjected. "I never said I did not believe you." Even I could hear that my voice had risen. "Ah," she exclaimed, "now we're talking. Of course my parents told me the story. How else would I know it?" I looked at her silently. "Why don't you ask me how my parents knew?" she went on. "You are dying to ask me. Don't you think my parents soon found out all there was to know about me and that criminal skipper friend of yours? Do you think they would make the story up? Do you think all those doctors would make the story up?"

'Drenched in icy cold sweat, I did not dare reply that most of the stories parents tell their children are made up. At last I understood what ignominious game Henry Pidgett had been playing all these years, loading the German scapegoat with all manner of deadly sins in order to exonerate himself of any responsibility in the tragedy that had befallen his family. I slid the starboard side door open and moved swiftly on to the side deck, just in time to retch over the rail. I could only hope that, under the cover of darkness, my spasms would remain unseen by my passengers. I was still bent over when I detected a throaty humming sound that seemed to get louder by the second and indeed soon almost drowned out our own engine noise. Next, this rumble was so loud that I looked up, half expecting to find a helicopter overhead. I scanned the horizon from port to starboard and from starboard to port, vainly searching for the lights of some craft, but the sea was pitch dark. I got back inside, reduced the radar range to one and a half miles and re-tuned it. There it was: a small but distinct echo moving fast across our port bow, hardly three hundred metres ahead. A quick computation showed that the unlit craft was travelling at about forty knots. Not only is such speed insane at night, but this craft also ignored all rules of the road, starting with the fact that we had right of way. "Did you hear that?" I asked. They nodded. Sixty seconds later *Gwelan II* pitched and rolled violently as we crossed the wake of the phantom vessel. Akzo nodded appreciatively and asked whether I had seen anything. I shook my head. "Big rigid inflatable," he said. "Seven, eight metres, with two big Honda outboard engines. Impossible to catch." "Friends of yours?" I asked. He beamed his irritating smile at me and threw his hands up.

'All the while I was desperately trying to make sense of Piggy's story. It couldn't be a coincidence – it had to be the same accident – but it was impossible for my brain to conceive that this vindictive freak could be – could be – could possibly be . . . my little Rose-Anne. In an attempt to dispel the nightmare, I tried to work out the dates. How long was it since the tragedy? Twenty-five – no, twenty-seven years. Rose-Anne was six at the time; today she would be thirty-three or thirty-four. Somehow, her birthday, which for so long I knew better than mine, was now eluding me. Could Piggy be only thirty-four? She could just as well be fifty. Or thirty. Come to think of it, none of the usual telltale signs were available – she was in a category all of her own, which nobody else could interpret. And whose behaviour probably was utterly unpredictable. On the other hand, I wasn't the only German skipper in the world, and many accidents must have occurred in these waters. But Lipari – she had mentioned Lipari – there couldn't be any doubt.

'"You see, Flying Dutchman," she croaked triumphantly, "your night vision isn't so important in these

176

parts, is it? There is nothing for people like you to see. You'd be no match for these brave Albanian sailors."

'I put a cheese platter on the table, hoping that she would eventually relent and concentrate on her food – but to no avail.

' "Do you know how long I have been looking for that German bugger?" she suddenly shouted. "All my life. All my bloody life! And I shall never stop. Believe me – we'll find him sooner or later – won't we, my love?" "I shoot German bugger," Akzo confirmed matter-of-factly. Piggy turned to me. "I bet you know him," she hissed, darting a piercing glance at me. "You lowlives spend your time hanging out together in bars and pubs, sharing dirty stories – don't you? I bet you've come across him. Wherever he's holed up – we'll find him. He can't hide for ever." Suddenly she threw her head back and started panting.

' "What was his name?" I asked as innocently as possible.

' "Werther – von – Ringsburg." She enunciated my name with almost sensuous precision. "Some kind of pretentious German aristocrat."

' "Why did your parents not stay in touch with him?" I asked. "Why did they not at the very least sue him?"

' "They tried. But I told you: the coward went into hiding. All the efforts made by my parents to find him came to nothing. To this day nobody has been able to trace him. Akzo has friends in all European countries, all well incentivised to find him: nothing. Besides, my parents had bigger problems anyway."

'I raised an interrogative eyebrow.

' "I don't suppose you know how this kind of tragedy tends to affect families," she went on. "Simple: it destroys them. When a child dies or is crippled, it is rare for the parents to stay together. Grief – the incommunicability of grief – what do you know about that? The repressed guilt. The anger at the whole fucking world – you wouldn't understand any of that. Couples just don't survive this sort of ordeal. Perhaps I ought to have died. They would have produced a couple more children and gone on, cherishing fond memories of their little angel. The silver-framed pictures of the blonde, sweet little thing I used to be would be plastered all over their sitting-room." She giggled. "I'm afraid I didn't oblige. Sorry. Very selfish of me. Only snag was, my parents couldn't cope. Seeing their lovely daughter damaged was too much. Not good for their self-image, I suppose. By the age of nine I was seeking solace in food. I started binging. I turned into a disgusting fat lump. By the time I was fourteen, I desperately hated school. Boys – the nicer ones – kept calling me fat and trying to trip me up in the corridors just for the fun of seeing my fat wobble. As for the more vicious ones – you can just imagine. I told my parents. I told my teachers. Nobody believed me. Nobody cared. I picked up some kitchen scissors. It was painful – but it felt good. The only thing that made me feel good. See?"

'She extended both arms. I saw. Hidden within the adipose folds, a criss-cross of fine lines and thick puckers covering the inside of her forearms and wrists like so many sickly wrinkles. Some discoloured, some pinkish.

Some straight, some jagged. There wasn't a square millimetre of healthy skin left. A pathetic mess. It made me feel sick. Sick with pity. Sick about myself. Sick about the whole sick world.

' "Why me?" she asked, looking at Akzo. "Why did they all hate me? It made no sense. Once I deliberately pushed the blades further in till I felt the veins – and pushed again. It takes time for all your blood to flow out: they found me. They saved me. Saved me! Ha! Returned me to hell, rather. Akzo, my love, you are the one that saved me – years later. At the time I plunged ever deeper into freakishness. Call it self-hatred if you will. Anyway it was too much for my parents. How could such self-centred people be expected to share what neither of them could bear? Soon my father distanced himself from us and started running after other women. The older he got, the younger they became. I hardly saw him for years – until I was alone." '

'My head was spinning so furiously that I nearly collapsed on the helm seat. Rose-Anne – my sweet, lovely baby – my Sea-Daughter – could *this* be you? What have they done to you? Where, inside the hateful volcano, are you hiding? How could this creature be the same as my little girl? I felt in my bones that she wasn't – yet my brain told me she was. I experienced no fear. For too long I had been beyond fear. Nausea, yes, and confusion, mixed up with overwhelming revulsion. The only thought that crossed my mind with any clarity was: Thank God Katharina is not here to witness this. It would have broken her heart. But I needed to hear the rest of the story.

' "Why were you alone?" I heard myself ask. "What happened to Camilla?"

'For a minute she said nothing. She just sat there, not even looking at me, gazing at the distant past, pondering the immediate future. Her hands were resting on the saloon table, holding her knife and fork vertically like two symmetrical candle holders. Her absolute immobility lent her a Buddha-like serenity. Pounding my temples, my pulse was racing so furiously that it almost drowned out the rumble of the slow-revving engines that were steadily propelling us towards the Albanian coast. Seated opposite Piggy, Akzo was munching a mixture of bread, goats' cheese in vine leaves and gleaming black olives, nodding frequently in a display of unreserved approval. He caught my eye, winked and again smiled.

' "Akzo, my love," Piggy said in a small voice, without looking at him, "did you hear what he just asked?"

'Akzo swallowed his mouthful, took a swig of beer and carefully wiped his mouth on the last paper napkin.

' "Of course I hear," he protested, sounding like the pupil caught napping at the back of the class. "He ask . . . he ask . . . what happen to Camilla!"

' "Precisely, my love," she confirmed in the same pensive, small voice. "Mr Kurt asked what happened to Camilla. But – *I never mentioned my mother's name.* How does Mr Kurt know it? Do you have any idea, my darling Akzo? Do you? Because – I think I have a pretty good idea myself. Methinks Mr Kurt isn't Mr Kurt. What do you think, my love?"

5

' The regular drone of the big diesel engines, far from
detracting from the stillness that had taken hold of
the saloon, only seemed to make it more tangible.

'As Piggy, her thin lips twisted by a faint smile,
pensively stared straight ahead at the large brass ship's
clock, I wondered whether she too was feeling that
mixture of lassitude and elation that comes at the end
of an exhausting quest. That both lifelong pursuits – I
searching for Katharina, Piggy hunting me down – were
manifestly over, curiously filled me with anticipation
more than dread. After a quarter of a century spent
wondering what had become of Rose-Anne, I had at
last stumbled on the answer – the terrible answer. These
broken lives, the unrealised promise of childhood – this
catalogue of damage and pain, rancour and misery, of
freefall into monstrosity – left me reeling under the
weight of my responsibility. Yet – at least the uncertainty
had gone. At long last I knew. I could now face the
cataclysmic consequences of the decision I had made, one

day in 1975, to drop anchor in Valle Muria. And though these consequences were more horrendous than the most unspeakable of my nightmares, somehow I knew that they would be easier to deal with. You know how we often are paralysed in nightmares. Poignant though Piggy's story of loss and suffering had been, it had freed me from my world of angry spectres, and transported me to a radically different place – no less hideous, but at least possessed of the hard edge of the real. She had returned me to an inexorable reality.

'It was Akzo who broke the spell. The gun was in his hand. A top-of-the-range, state-of-the-art semi-automatic Smith and Wesson.

' "I shoot German bugger?" he asked.

'Piggy came out of her reverie.

' "I think I'll do it myself," she answered. "Give me the gun."

'Without taking his eyes off me, Akzo put the gun in her hand.

' "You know how shoot?" he asked.

'She nodded. Just as he was taking the safety catch off, the radio started crackling. We were keeping watch on Channel 16, where the Italian coastguard were announcing that a full weather forecast would follow on Channel 68. I automatically lifted the handset to switch channels, when Piggy suddenly barked: "Stop!" The dark mouth of the gun was steadily staring at me. "Put it down – immediately!" she hissed. I slowly put the handset back on to its wall-mounted cradle. "Now – listen carefully," she went on. "I want you to pick up that radio again – very carefully. Make absolutely sure you don't accidentally press the 'talk' button. Then rip the wire from the wall and give Akzo the handset."

'I did as she asked. "Akzo, my darling," she said, "have you seen the portable radio by the rear door?" He nodded. "Go and fetch it," she commanded. He obeyed, and tried in vain to slide my portable VHF into his trouser pocket, which was far too small. Eventually, he somehow managed to fit it into his empty pistol holster. I took a couple of slow steps back to the helm and, out of habit, scanned the horizon. The night was moonless; if there had been any traffic within ten miles, their lights would have been easy to pick up against the pitch-black darkness. There wasn't a single light in sight. Which does not mean the sea was empty, of course. Sometimes people talk of an empty sea, but this is inaccurate. The sea is never empty. It is replete with truth. And brimming with souls running away from the truth.'

Suddenly Kurt stopped and looked at me. I was caught completely off-guard. Truth! Only last week Sarah, my lover, had the cheek to ask me how I could go back home every evening and live a lie. I had skirted around the question. The obvious answer was that it was because of her. The alternative would have been to explain to her that I wasn't living a lie, that the ties that bind me to Cathy and Lucy are real and solid. Instead I reminded her that we lawyers earn our living distorting the truth to the advantage of our clients. Even doctors lie most of the time. They never truthfully tell you how painful a procedure is going to be, how long you'll need to recover, or what your chances of survival are, or how long you have to live. Soon after my discussion with Sarah, I tackled Cathy on this issue. Of course she disagreed. 'Truth is what works for my patients,' she'd said. 'And, to a large extent, what works for my patients is what they want to hear. Anything else would harm them – and therefore is unacceptable to a doctor.' Pragmatic truth, I think it is called. On her own terms, I guess I was truthful in hiding from her a liaison that would hurt her.

Kurt was still staring at me expectantly.

'How the hell should I know what's in the briny?' I mumbled. 'Back to your story: what happened when you told Rose-Anne your version of events – and how sorry you were for that accident?'

'I didn't get a chance to do so,' Kurt replied. 'Before I could gather my wits, Piggy asked: "Now, Mr Kurt, would you like to tell us exactly where we are? Please make it very clear, so that even stupid landlubbers like us can understand."

'I had a quick look at the chart plotter and told her we were some seventy nautical miles out of Durres.

'"When shall we arrive?" she asked.

'I explained that at our current speed, we'd need some nine hours; however, we could increase speed at first light, thus cutting our travelling time to seven or eight hours. It was close to midnight, so we'd make Durres in the early morning.

'"Akzo," she said, still pointing the gun at me, "can you drive this boat into Durres and dock there?"

'"I can drive boat," he answered. "But . . . this boat

no inflatable dinghy. Also, many minefields on approaches to Durres. When we get close to Durres I call my friend on radio." He tapped his bulging hip. "My friend they come with speedboat and help us."

'Akzo was right about Durres. It is the main port of Albania, and serves the capital, Tirana, but its approaches were heavily mined during the Second World War and never properly cleared since. The only cleared channel, on heading 018 degrees, surrounded by shoals and wrecks, is tricky at the best of times and particularly hazardous in poor visibility.

' "Fine," Piggy said. "The so-called Mr Kurt will be delighted to guide us through the approaches of Durres, since this revised plan increases his life expectancy by a huge factor, from one minute to several hours in fact – won't you, dear Mr Kurt?"

'I shrugged.

' "Aren't skippers supposed to be good at mental calculation?" she whined. "They must be. Professional skippers are good at everything – aren't they? . . . I'll tell you what. Suppose that, instead of shooting you in sixty seconds, like the dog you are, I granted you life for another eight hours – how many times longer would you then live? You have five seconds to show me your mental prowess. Only one answer. Get it wrong and I'll shoot you. We can't have incompetent skippers on our boat – not with all those minefields ahead – can we, my love?"

'An air of anticipation on his smooth face, Akzo enthusiastically shook his head. Fixing me through narrowed pupils, she started counting.

' "One."

'I gazed at her in utter wonderment, still hoping to find a sparkle of recognition, a streak of humanity.

' "Two."

'I did not mind dying at the hand of Rose-Anne. But this freak? Who the hell did she think she was?

' "Three."

'Nothing. There was no chink in this armour of vileness, no trace of the happy little girl who had once loved me, no sign of any emotion in the steady hands which, resting on the table, kept the Smith and Wesson firmly pointed in my direction. Two thoughts crossed my mind: it seemed it was a 9mm calibre, and she was likely to hit me in the belly. Instinctively, I bent my knees to try and receive the bullet in the chest. Far less messy.

' "Four."

'How many minutes in seven hours? Or was it eight hours? Four hundred and forty minutes? Who cared? Katharina, I love you. I have always loved you. Forgive me, Katharina.

' "Four hundred and eighty times," I said as she counted five.

'Pause.

'She seemed disappointed.

' "You're getting awfully slow in your old age, skipper," she relented. "But what's agreed is agreed. You're lucky that Akzo and I are honourable people. Now then, we might as well make ourselves comfortable for the rest of this most pleasant cruise. Akzo, my love, I think Mr Kurt would be much more relaxed with his hands and feet tied. It would help him concentrate on his navigation, and eliminate any distracting thoughts from his mind."

'Akzo went up the companionway to fetch a rope. Though he astutely selected the thinnest line he could find, when he returned he did not find the job easy. First, the diameter of that polyester rope, designed to hold a thirty-tonne boat, was fairly substantial; second, it wasn't particularly supple; and last, there were ten or twelve metres of it. He tried his best, though, and I winced a couple of times as he tugged wildly to tighten the knots up. At the end both my wrists and feet had disappeared behind the twisted polyester, whilst being joined in such a way that I couldn't stand straight.

' "Very sexy, Mr von Ringsburg," Piggy grated, "very sexy indeed. It doesn't look like you will be molesting little girls tonight, does it? Tough old life, isn't it? Very sorry about that. Please accept our most sincere apologies for not being able to satisfy your depraved instincts."

'Her voice had become shriller again, and she was waving the gun at me, waiting for an answer that did not come. Suddenly she began shouting.

' "Talking of apologies – you fucking swine – have you got nothing to say? Look at me! Bloody look at me! Have you got *nothing* to say?"

'She was sweating and panting, on the verge of hyperventilation, the matt black gun trembling in her hand. She was likely to press the trigger at any time, if only by accident – unless I could say something to placate her, but there was nothing to say, there was too much to say – anyway words failed me. What can you say, when you don't even know who you are talking to? How could I tell her that her parents were dastardly liars without provoking even greater fury? I kept looking at her, as she had ordered; she was holding my gaze, and second after second came and went, each of which I expected to be my last. Akzo slowly got up, moved next to her and began to massage her neck. All of a sudden she turned away.

'"All right," she sighed. "I guess that child abusers have serious problems with the truth, don't they? Now Akzo, my love, I think we need to get organised for the night. This German arsehole needs watching. If you're happy to start, I'll go and get some sleep now. Make sure you call me as soon as you feel tired."

'Without taking her little eyes off me, she gave him the gun.

'No problem,' Akzo acquiesced. 'You sleep well. I shoot German bugger if he moves finger.'

'"That's the spirit," she said, patting his free hand. "Don't talk to him. And don't let him talk to you. If he opens his filthy mouth – shoot him."

'"I shoot German bugger in filthy mouth and ass," Akzo volunteered.

'Struggling to extricate mounds of flesh wedged underneath, Piggy, in her unseemly attempt to get up, almost ripped the table off its single central stainless-steel pillar. When she finally succeeded, she stood there for a minute, catching her breath, mountainous, magnificent, more maleficent than ever; then, one step at a time, holding on to the grab rails, she limped towards the aft cabin and slammed the door shut.

' "Don't think play tricks – or you dead meat," Akzo cheerfully advised, waving his gun under my nose. The inscription on the barrel read *Performance Center 952* or something like that.

'I didn't answer, choosing instead to concentrate on what was likely to be my last night watch. I was disappointed that the matter had not yet been brought to a conclusion. I was more than ready for the bullet that had eluded me for so long. There was poetic justice in Rose-Anne being my executioner, and, above all, I was happy to die at sea. Rather than rotting in some African swamp, at least my body would enjoy the watery grave of sirens, mermaids and true mariners. Above all, I was tired. Given the suffering I had caused, my quest for Katharina was now pointless; never could we face up to what we had unwittingly engendered. Had she known? Suddenly I was struck by the certainty that Katharina somehow had come across the unspeakable, and run away not for her sake – but for mine. Would I ever want to tell her the horror that our Sea-Daughter had become? No, no and no; I would have protected her from that deadly knowledge with my own life.

'I felt such intolerable sadness that I wondered how I could end it all swiftly. I could pretend to attack Akzo; however, given the fact that my hands and feet were tied, he probably wouldn't feel sufficiently threatened to shoot me. Most probably he would thump me on the head, which wouldn't achieve much. I could also jump overboard as soon as he dozed off; since swimming would be impossible, this would guarantee a swift end. On the other hand, I wasn't sure about Akzo's ability to navigate the boat safely to port. I was still the skipper in charge, and felt strangely reluctant to let Rose-Anne down again. Indeed, if my death was to be of any use, she should neither be cheated of her vengeance nor deprived of its therapeutic benefits. The third option involved following her script, navigating through the Durres minefields and being put down like a dog on arrival. Whatever pride was left in me rebelled against such an inglorious end, but I reasoned this was the only death which would in any way benefit my Sea-Daughter, and that it would be no worse than the gratuitous one I had so avidly been seeking from Congolese battlefields to Rwandan minefields.

'I was still undecided when, out of the corner of my eye, I caught what seemed to be a light on our starboard beam. First I thought it was a reflection on the saloon window; but when I moved my head in order to look straight out of the open door to my right, it was still there. I couldn't quite make out whether it was fixed, occulting or flashing; whilst it sometimes disappeared, it displayed no recognisable rhythm or pattern. If it were a buoy or some low floating object, its irregular periods of extinction could have been explainable by its dropping down to the trough of the swell, thus momentarily falling out of sight. Its colour was a pale yellow, which ruled out any shipping, since boats, as you know, carry green and red sidelights together with white masthead and stern lanterns. This was the oddest thing about it: if it was not on a boat, it had to be some kind of navigational aid or beacon, a special mark, some cardinal mark – but that made no sense whatsoever, since we were in the middle of the sea, sixty nautical miles from the nearest land. Not only is there no need for marks in such waters, since there is nothing worth marking, but also they could not possibly be positioned, since the sea is far too deep. Just to make sure, I checked on my chart, which predictably showed no navigation mark, lit or unlit, in the clear waters between the Italian and Albanian coasts. I remembered that hydrofoils and seaplanes carry fast-flashing orange lights, and wondered whether one of those might have caught up with us. But first, that orange flashing light should be shown in addition to all normal running lamps, not by itself; second, the luminescence I was watching stayed in exactly the same place in relation to us, which indicated that it was travelling on a parallel course at exactly the same slow speed as us; last it was neither fast-flashing nor orange, but pale and erratic – and utterly mystifying. With great difficulty, I picked up my field glasses and had a good look. Akzo immediately became agitated. "What are you looking at, German bugger? I shoot now if play game."

'I gave him the glasses, closed my eyes, rubbed them against my polyester ties and re-opened them. Still there. This glow did not seem to be a figment of my imagination; yet, in the surrounding darkness, there was no shape or silhouette, nothing next to it. I could not even decide whether it was a faint radiance near to us or a bright one very far away. "Tell me what you see," I told

Akzo, nodding to starboard. He scanned the horizon and finally trained the glasses on the mysterious gleam. "I see light," he said. "Must be boat there."

'Of course he had to be right. It had to be some kind of local embarkation, maybe one of those small fishing craft that, in complete disdain of all regulations, only carry some sort of *ad hoc* lantern, torch lamp or whatever. Certainly not a *lamparo*, though; this powerful gas burner used by Sicilians to attract fish by night is dazzlingly luminous, it can be clearly identified from a distance of several miles – and it has no occultations. I had a look at my radar screen, which was set on my normal cruising range of twelve nautical miles, expecting to see a blob on our starboard beam. Nothing. I realised that such a craft was probably too small and near to be picked up on such a big range, so I reduced the range to six miles and waited. Nothing. I reduced it again to three miles, and waited. Nothing. I pressed the target expansion button. Nothing, not the faintest echo. Increasing the gain just produced masses of confused interference: I turned it down again. Ignoring Akzo, who was suspiciously breathing down my neck, Smith and Wesson at the ready, I repeated the procedure down to one and a half miles, then again on the shortest range, three-quarters of a mile. My reliable Raytheon radar stubbornly refused to pick up any object on our starboard beam – or anywhere else for that matter. This convinced me that the light had to be some kind of optical illusion, since, on reduced range, my radar was perfectly capable of picking up objects as small as navigational buoys. Indeed I had more than once relied on its capabilities to thread my way through a maze of navigational marks when the thickest fog had closed visibility down to a boat's length. But this time it was categorical: there was nothing but water all around us. When I looked up again, I was expecting the light to have disappeared – yet it was still there, in exactly the same position. Then I understood. This was no vessel. The fact that its relative position never changed proved that it was some kind of reflection of our own lights. Any real object would either fall behind, if stationary, or move about, if it was making way. I leant forward and turned off all our navigation lights. Then I closed my eyes again, this time for several seconds. I re-opened them, and slowly scanned the horizon from port to starboard.

'It was still there.

'And it stayed in exactly the same position for the next hour, seemingly travelling at the same speed as us.

'I searched my mind for a few lines by Kierkegaard I'd once learnt by heart, but their precise wording now escaped me . . . something to do with strange lights in the sea and souls about to part from bodies.

'Yet, as soon as I stopped trying to solve the puzzle, I felt oddly comforted by this dim glow. Whatever was accompanying me on my last night watch wasn't hostile; on the contrary, it was so inviting that I had to restrain myself not to dive in head first to investigate it at close range.

'Having long given up trying to identify this travelling companion, I was even in danger of dozing off under its protection when it dawned on me that there might in fact be some kind of pattern to its occultations. Perhaps I was making it all up – yet it now seemed to me that, every fifteen seconds or so, it went off for a longish while. Then, when it reappeared, it first showed two long flashes; then, one quick one; then, a long one between two short ones.'

Kurt stopped to draw breath.

'Morse code,' I said. 'What does it mean?'

'Well, if it was Morse, I guess it read M-E-R,' he replied dreamily. 'M-E-R, M-E-R, M-E-R repeated for hours on my starboard beam, in the middle of an empty sea.'

'But – what does it mean?' Cathy echoed.

'I do not know,' he whispered. 'What do you think?'

Cathy shrugged her shoulders.

'French for *sea*?' she suggested.

'Who knows?' Kurt said. 'Did I tell you that Katharina used to call me her Mer-King? Well – it might have been a coincidence – for the first time in all those years, I now sensed her presence. I mean – I strongly felt her *physical* presence, quite close. Her inviting, loving presence. Suddenly I felt at peace, all longing gone, fulfilled in the knowledge that at last I had been reunited with my wife, made whole again, and that . . . my life had been worth living. Whatever fear of dying I might have been harbouring was gone; and all fear of living too.'

Cathy, who had been shivering for a while, interrupted Kurt.

'My God . . . Kurt . . . this is incredible,' she cried.

'I know,' he apologised. 'It was the middle of the night, I was mentally and physically exhausted, and you must believe that I had fallen prey to delusions. So be it. I am not trying to convince you.'

'You don't understand,' Cathy cried. 'Your love . . . your love for Katharina . . . that's incredibly beautiful . . . Terence – isn't it just wonderful?'

Puzzled that my wife, a medical doctor, should almost be reduced to tears by a confused story about unidentified flashing lights, I patted her hands in a silent attempt to comfort her. It is a sad fact that more Westerners now believe in alien abduction than believe in the theory of evolution; but Cathy and I used to share the same contempt for astrology, telepathy, flying saucers, religious miracles and other occult phenomena. Admittedly, she now was too tired to think clearly, and it is easy to get women worked up about love. For my part, I wasn't going to be drawn into this digression. Better to stick to the facts and try and get to the end of the story.

The darkness around us had somehow thinned sufficiently for me to perceive that Kurt and Cathy were looking at each other with intense concentration.

'I'm sorry we interrupted,' I said.

Kurt slowly turned away from Cathy.

'You've heard all that matters,' he replied quietly. 'The rest can be told quickly. What's the time?'

'Nearly four,' I answered.

'That's right,' he said. 'It was just before four o'clock that my light faded away. Despite its extinction, I remained at peace, filled with enough serene confidence to last me for the rest of my life. I knew that Katharina had forgiven me. I knew she wanted me to forgive myself and live. Live.

'I told Akzo I needed to relieve myself. Having duly indicated to me which parts of my anatomy would be blown off if I got up to any tricks, he let me slowly hop over to the aft deck, and stood watching me in the frame of the aft saloon door. I went right up to the starboard quarter, in the hope of perhaps catching a last glimpse of luminescence behind us, but the horizon remained stubbornly dark – until, on our port side, many miles away, I distinguished the faint running lights of a ship. My attempts to open my fly were thwarted by the thickness of the many layers of rope that encircled my wrists. I hopped back to Akzo and explained the problem. "You piss in trousers!" he laughed. When I asked him to demonstrate the procedure, he relented and untied my hands. "You hurry," he said. "Perhaps Piggy she wake up." I thanked him and hopped back to the port quarter. Without any doubt there was a substantial ship out there, her two masthead lights indicating an overall length over fifty metres. Could have been anything. A container ship, a bulk freighter, an oil tanker. Whilst looking, I realised that I was standing next to the locker in which I keep safety equipment, such as U-rings, fire extinguisher and flares. Perhaps this was the point when my re-awakened survival instinct took over. The point where my body rebelled and started its undignified struggle for self-preservation.'

He turned to Cathy.

'You must have seen people die – you will know how hard, how long their body will fight for one more, one last, one hopeless gasp.'

Cathy nodded.

'Under cover of darkness,' he resumed, 'I lifted the top of the locker. On an impulse, I grabbed a pack of flares, opened it, and, in the dark, selected the biggest cylinder, which I expected to be a red parachute rocket. I have already mentioned how they work: they shoot up to a height of three hundred metres, open their parachute, fire their powerful red flare, and slowly drift down over several minutes, thus maximising their chances of attracting attention. With no calculated plan in my head, I guess I felt this was my last chance, since we'd soon be in Albanian waters. Just as I had taken the cap off the flare and was pulling out its safety pin, Akzo got suspicious. "What you up to, Mr Kurt?" he asked. I hardly heard him move forward a couple of steps before he shone a blinding torchlight into my face. "I shoot ass!" he shouted, raising his gun. With my feet tied, I couldn't have gone anywhere – anyway, before I could even think of ducking or jumping overboard he'd fired. I don't know what he was aiming at. What I know is that the flare fired off straight into his foot, bounced against the bulwark next to the door and crashed into the sea, where it hissed and growled for several seconds before reluctantly fizzling out. It may be that the bullet had actually hit my hand, or perhaps I had pressed the trigger of the flare in a reflex action when he shot. Of course I wasn't ready for firing the thing; indeed, instead of holding the plastic handle I was holding its metallic body – with the result you have seen.'

Cathy had regained her composure.

'I understand,' she said. 'My guess is that the bullet hit you, taking off the best part of your little finger and ring finger; as for the rest of the mess, which is worse, it clearly was caused by some kind of flame-thrower.'

'You're the doctor. As I mentioned, these things burn at a temperature of 1,800 degrees Fahrenheit: you certainly don't want to hold them in your hand. Anyway, whether due to the shock, the impact or a combination of both, Akzo, screaming his head off, fell backwards down the companionway, his trousers in flames. For a while I stood there, dazed and blinded by the flare. It took a few seconds for the pain in my hand to appear and rise to ever more excruciating levels. Damage assessment was hampered by darkness, but the overpowering stench of burnt flesh told its own story. What surprised me was that the wound seemed to be bleeding profusely, since I would have expected it to be cauterised by the burn; of course, I did not know then that part of it had been caused by a bullet. Just before my knees gave way, I sat down on the locker and tried to compose myself. I remembered that burns are sterile, and therefore should not be dressed with non-sterile material; yet it immediately became obvious that I needed to stem the bleeding. My first-aid kit was in the forward cabin; accessing it, or anything else inside the boat, would have made me into a sitting duck and probably attracted fire. I could hear complete mayhem inside the saloon. Piggy had been woken up by the commotion; there was banging and shouting, and smoke was escaping from the saloon door. I couldn't see it in the dark, but it was thick enough to make me cough, though I was sitting several yards away near the stern. Sitting in a pool of blood, I thought of the rags I keep in a locker on the flying-bridge to clean the stainless steel and decided to fetch them to dress my wound. This was a risky move, because the flying-bridge is a cul-de-sac. Should Akzo or Piggy come out looking for me when I was up there, I would be trapped. My chances of survival were better on the main deck, particularly with Akzo injured. If I could free my legs, I could try to play hide and seek, circling back and forth from the aft deck to the foredeck as he chased me. Of course that would depend on total darkness, since, at dawn, he would not only be able to see me, but also to shoot through the big windows and windscreen. A smallish boat is essentially a confined space, with no hiding place. I reckoned the sun would rise within the hour, thus putting an end to the game – unless Akzo first thought of flooding the decks with lights, which of course was possible if he found the right circuit breakers.

'First I needed to untie my feet, which I did with the help of my pocket knife. Tiptoeing as lightly as I could, I made my way across the aft deck and up the flying-bridge ladder. The pain caused by the contact between coarse dirty rags and the exposed ends of my nerves almost made me faint. Since I couldn't tolerate the slightest pressure on the wound, my improvised dressing proved quite ineffectual to contain the haemorrhage; the only noticeable improvement was that the material soaked up some of the blood which otherwise would have kept spurting all over the place. I carefully wrapped the whole mess in as many layers as possible and tied them up loosely with my left hand. This was the best I could do, and I didn't want to prolong my stay up there.

'On my way down, I was struck by the thought that I could use the controls on the flying-bridge helm station at least to stop the boat – or perhaps change our course back towards Italy. I sat down at the helm, switched off the autopilot, hesitated for a moment – and put it back on. Any change I initiated from here could not only be immediately countermanded from the lower helm station inside the saloon, but would also betray my presence on the flying-bridge. Too risky. I went down the ladder and stood next to the aft saloon door, listening. Because all the curtains were drawn, I couldn't see inside. There was still pandemonium down below, but no more smoke coming out of the door, just an acrid smell of burnt plastic and barbecued flesh. Piggy was alternately shouting and wailing, but Akzo's voice was too low for me to detect more than a faint rumble. Both of them seemed to be down in the galley, probably because this seemed the natural place to fight a fire. Not only was tap water available, but there were also a fire blanket on the wall next to the cooker and a fire extinguisher opposite it, which I had demonstrated to them during my pre-departure safety briefing.

'I felt sorry for the blond lad who had unwittingly been caught in this long-running tragedy, and wondered what they would do next. Perhaps they had decided to wait for daybreak before coming after me. If they had another gun in their luggage, the hunt would be over in seconds: Akzo only had to wait in ambush anywhere, whilst Piggy went round the boat, or vice versa. Alternatively, perhaps they had already alerted their friends on my portable radio; though its range was less than twenty miles, we were getting ever closer to Albania. One way or the other the situation looked grim. I decided that I had to stop the boat's inexorable progression, since my position would hardly improve with hordes of Albanian hoodlums on board. I also had to make it impossible for Akzo and Piggy to override my actions. How?

'Simple: I had to turn both engines off and throw the keys overboard.

'On reflection, not so simple: this had to be performed from the lower helm station inside the saloon, where the keys were. This was complicated by the fact that all the inside lights were now on, so that I would be fully exposed. If Akzo or Piggy were standing in the middle of the galley, they wouldn't even need to climb up the five steps leading to the saloon to shoot me: I would immediately be in their line of fire. Unless I crouched under the helmsman's seat, and then, keeping my head down, stopped the engines and got the keys out solely by feel. With two hands, that plan was just about realistic; with only my left hand, much more time would be needed, first to throttle both engines back, then press both "Stop" switches, then recover both ignition keys – without even being able to see the dashboard. Another risk was that, in spite of not seeing me, they would simply spray the helm's position with bullets; without any doubt, the flimsy plywood and teak veneer of the helm seat would afford me next to no protection. On the other hand, they might assume I was driving the boat from the flying-bridge and rush out to catch me up there.

'If my chances of surviving an incursion into the illuminated saloon weren't high, what were the alternatives? Jumping ship clearly was one. There were three ways to do this. First, I could simply jump in the briny and rely on my life jacket to support me until I got picked up. This plan had several drawbacks: the Adriatic is vast and I might never be rescued; also, given my weakened condition and loss of blood, I probably wouldn't survive for more than a few hours, even in those relatively warm waters; last, if rescue did eventually turn up in time, it was more than likely to be in the form of potentially hostile Albanians. Both other options involved lowering some kind of craft into the water. The choice was between the liferaft and the rigid inflatable dinghy we used as tender. I soon discarded the liferaft: it is designed for eight people, and its container weighs some eighty kilos. It was impossible for me to lift it and throw it overboard with only one hand. This left the tender, which could be lowered from the davits without much effort. Although our davits are manual, not electrical, they are quite easy to operate, and craning such a light dinghy up or down could be done one-handedly. This was by far the best option – except for a fatal flaw. No tender has ever been launched from a moving boat, and it is impossible to do so. The normal procedure, as you realise, is to crane the dinghy down to the water and then to release the two steel cables that hold it under the davits. Of course, this can only be done after the weight of the tender has been taken off these cables. But, if I lowered the dinghy from a speeding boat, as soon as it hit the water it would start dragging, keeping the cables too taut for release. Only after *Gwelan II* had stopped could I hope to release the tender.

'So I was almost back to square one – but not quite. I resolved to lower the tender almost down to the water and leave it dangling on its cables; then I had to attempt stopping the boat. If I succeeded, I would run back to the stern, lower the tender the last few centimetres into the water and release the now slack cables. Since I would only be able to operate one oar, it would take time, during which I would be exposed to fire, for me to get away from the yacht. I would have to rely on the last remnants of darkness – which meant making my move immediately.

'In reality, the combination of darkness and the loss of one hand hindered me so much that it took me the best part of fifteen minutes to lower that tender. By the time I had finished I could see that the darkness to the east was looking subtly different. This did not bode well for my escape plan, but the only thing I could do was to press on with it.

'As I made my way forward on the starboard side deck, towards the door that is fortunately located right next to the saloon helm position, the noises coming from down below had abated. I wondered what could be going on inside, but there was no way to find out, short of taking a peep, which would have been reckless. I was crouching outside the door, listening for any sound that might betray the location of my two passengers, when I picked up a familiar rumble. Once again it turned into a roar and quickly built up to a deafening climax as some kind of craft, aiming almost straight at us, thundered across our bows. All the while I was wondering whether it signalled the arrival of Akzo's friends but, far from slowing down, it simply sped away as fast as it had appeared. I recognised the engines' racket: it was the very machine that had crossed our path earlier on, going in the opposite direction. This time I saw a slightly luminescent streak where otherwise invisible light particles collided with the foam and spray thrown up in its wake, but again caught no glimpse of the actual vessel. I couldn't understand why smugglers, instead of giving legitimate traffic a wide berth – after all, we could have been some law-enforcement patrol boat – should repeatedly cut across our bows at the risk of hitting us. Sheer bravado? Intimidation? Or incompetence? Maybe they assumed that, unlike us, customs boats and other coast-guard craft would patrol unlit, so that we were bound to be innocuous. Anyway, before I knew it, we were once again hit by the bow wave of the mysterious craft. This time, however, *Gwelan II* was rocked even more violently. In the dark, it was hard to guess exactly what caused the commotion; it may have been due to the angle at which we hit the maelstrom, or the speedboat's wake may have accidentally combined with the increasing swell to produce a roguishly steep wave, or the mysterious craft might have been travelling even faster than on the first occasion; be that as it may, although I was expecting a bump, I lost my balance and, from my crouching position, found myself on my back, sliding aft along the side deck. Simultaneously I heard a massive thwack inside the saloon. Only after a couple of metres could I grab the lower rail with my good hand and stop the slide. My injured right hand had hit something on the way, pain shooting through it so viciously that my vision blurred. I sat there for a couple of minutes, catching my breath and wondering what could have been thrown about inside the boat. When I finally got up, strange grunting noises were coming from the starboard saloon door. I slowly walked back up to it and resumed my crouching position, listening. The sound seemed to stem from the galley. This was a relief, since my plan would have been void had either Piggy or Akzo been in the saloon. The grunting steadily grew more intense – and still I could make no sense of it. Soon it became accompanied by moans, groans and wails, as well as intermittent flapping noises. It was clear that Piggy was the main, and possibly the only, source of noise. *They were having sex?* Notwithstanding her husband's injuries, the sex-crazed freak had somehow coerced him into copulation. My initial incredulity was swept aside by the wild crescendo of sobs and wails now emanating from the galley. This was my chance. An opportunity to stop the engines, get the keys and retreat before they showered me with bullets. I made my move when Piggy's moans and grunts reached an almost hysterical tempo. Standing outside for a couple of seconds, I tried to memorise the exact location of all the controls; then, doubled up, I slid into the saloon, protected by the helmsman's bench. I caught my breath, counted to three and went for it. First the throttles, on the port side. Easy: they are big, and I could use my left hand. I throttled the engines back to tick-over speed; their deep rumble died down immediately, so that Piggy's panting sounded even more frantic. Then the gear levers, on the starboard side. Easy to find too, but tricky, since my right hand was inoperative; I had to try and extend my left arm beyond its natural limit without exposing my shoulder to possible incoming fire. By now Piggy was screaming her head off. Both gear levers to neutral. Next, the two "Stop" buttons. Those proved much more difficult to locate by touch only. Where the hell was the port one? Just as I thought I might have to put my head over the parapet and, at great risk to myself, have a peep, my fingers finally found it. Port engine off. Piggy was now fighting for breath and even invoking my name in confused curses. Starboard "Stop" button now identified. At last. Starboard engine off. Piggy now completely out of breath. Part of me couldn't help marvel at the wondrous orgasm the mountainous woman was experiencing. But I had already been playing with the dashboard for an eternity, and was expecting a hail of bullets any second now. Without doubt the lovebirds were now aware of the fact that both engines had stopped. Port engine key out.

Again, starboard ignition key incredibly difficult to reach, due to useless right hand. Got it – starboard ignition key out. I'd done it! I swiftly retreated to the side deck, stood up, breathed a few deep gasps of relief and threw both engine keys overboard, waiting for the shooting to begin and ready to duck if it proved erratic.

'There was no shooting. Only muffled commotion.

'Whenever the thumping stopped, *Gwelan II* drifted in complete silence, gently caressed by the lightest of breezes. There was no mistaking the pinkish glow that illuminated the eastern skies before spreading upwards, a harbinger of another scorching day. Looking forward, I saw the dim silhouette of the Delta anchor slowly materialise out of the darkness on our bowsprit. I had to make my escape. I was puzzled, though, that my raid on the saloon helm position had caused no reaction, and remained wary of a trap. It was possible, after all, that they were waiting for me, ready to take pot-shots at me as soon as I returned to the aft deck in order to finish lowering the tender. At first light, I would be exposed, and therefore needed to locate my opponents before making any move. I dropped to my knees and stuck my head back inside the side deck saloon door. Piggy now seemed to be wailing and intermittently crying for help. Yes, she was even calling me – imploring me to come to her rescue. Eventually, her weakening voice and breathless sobs convinced me that her distress might be real. There was no sound from Akzo. Puzzled, I cautiously moved my head, almost at floor level, beyond the protection of the helm's bench, to have a peek. They were nowhere to be seen. I could see all the way aft across the saloon, down the passage at the centre of the galley and even through the open door to the aft cabin – but neither Piggy nor Akzo. They had to be hiding somewhere. I smelt an ambush – yet her cries, which seemed to originate from the galley, sounded genuine – unless she was acting as a decoy, trying to lure me into revealing my whereabouts? I waited for a few minutes, trying to make sense of the situation. By then there was enough light to see a dolphin from fifty metres, and my escape plan looked perilous.

'I tiptoed across the saloon, aware that I had no chance should either of them suddenly appear at the foot of the five steps leading down to the galley. Between asthmatic wheezes, Piggy was now sobbing and faintly calling my name.

'First I saw her foot. Her deck shoe was on.

'On the starboard side of our galley we have what we call a dinette: that is, a small table in front of an L-shaped bench on which three or four people can sit. Piggy's foot indicated that she was lying on her back on the short side of the L, head near the backrest and feet near the passage at the bottom of the steps. I took another cautious step forward and saw that her dangling legs were agitated by spasms. She was fully clothed. Her right hand was weakly flapping about, banging against or perhaps trying to grab the table under which she seemed firmly en- sconced. The gun – the gun was lying on the floor, under the table. I was pretty sure I could get to it before her, but I still hadn't located Akzo. Most likely he was seated on the bench in the inside corner, thus invisible from where I stood. With Piggy exhibiting such extreme distress, I wondered what he could possibly be up to; perhaps his injuries had been more severe than I thought. Anyway, if he was indeed sitting in that corner, he was on the wrong side of the table with regard to the gun; with an injured leg, he was unlikely to beat me to it, particularly since I had the advantage of surprise. I made my move.

'I jumped down the five steps in one go – banging my head against the low ceiling in the process – landed next to the gun, kicked it towards the sink with my left foot, picked it up and immediately backed off, aiming at the amorphous mass behind the table. I could only hope that the safety catch was off, since, with only one hand, I couldn't have released it myself.

'Still lying on her back, waving both hands, Piggy was now imploring: "Please . . . Quick . . . Please . . ."

'It wasn't before I took a careful step forward that the full horror of the situation sank in.

'Since they both had their clothes on, I immediately saw that my initial assessment of their wild racket had been wide of the mark.

'She must have fallen backwards on to the bench when we were rocked by the speedboat, wedging herself between table and bulwark so deeply and tightly that she was caught like a tuna in a Sicilian death chamber. At the best of times, she would have been unable to sit up by sheer use of abdominal force; here, with nothing to pull against, tightly jammed under the tabletop, she was as doomed as an overturned turtle.

'But this wasn't the worst. Behind the table, I could now see Akzo's abdomen, legs and left foot. His right leg – the one where the foot was largely missing – had made an awful mess all around. Dark blood, strips of burnt flesh and half-molten material from his shoes and trousers were sprayed all over the wall, the tabletop and the bench cushions – as though he'd been lashing out in all directions. The smell was intolerable. He was lying lengthwise on the long side of the L-bench, perpendicular to Piggy, also on his back. The reason I could see neither his face nor chest was that she was lying on top of them. All of a sudden, the emergency became clear: he was trapped underneath her. Nobody could have breathed in that position. Not a single gasp. She was cutting off his oxygen supply as absolutely as if he were at the bottom of the sea.

'I threw the gun on the table, grabbed her extended hand and pulled hard. Nothing happened. The combination of her weight, her exhaustion and the resistance of the tabletop was too much for my left hand. Positioning my feet against the drawer at the bottom of the bench, I took a better grasp of her wrist. "You must help me," I gasped. "On the count of three." This time, buttressing myself against the low drawer and co-ordinating my pulling with her desperate grunts, I barely managed to lift her, but couldn't free her; soon, out of breath and covered in sweat, I had to let go. Piggy was stuck, and I had no forceps. She was now emitting a kind of steady, moaning whine. Unspeakable though it was, the thought that this hard labour was doomed to result in a stillbirth flashed through my mind. I was reliving the nightmare of all those years ago, when I had fought so hard to save my beloved Rose-Anne from drowning – but this time it was even worse. Worse because I was failing her *for the second time*. Back in Valle Muria, fearless and self-assured, I had unthinkingly carried out the rescue procedures I had been trained to perform in such an emergency. At that time, I had seized her extended hand, snatched her from her marine universe and forcibly brought her up to a brutal reality. Twenty-seven years later, as I racked my brains to find a way to lift her, I was filled with dread. In my enfeebled state, I had no chance of lifting her twenty or twenty-five stone all by myself. She had to free herself. I threw myself down on my knees and frantically started to winch the table up. Exactly like the saloon table, this one could be lowered or lifted on its single stainless-steel central leg depending on whether the bench behind it was to be used as a berth or a seat. Cranking the handle at maximum speed, I overshot the top of the pillar, with the result that the tabletop, pushed from below by Piggy, shot up into the air and crashed first on to Akzo's legs before coming to rest on the floor, taking the gun and a couple of tumblers with it. Even freed from the table, she was now too weak to sit up by herself, but within seconds I had pulled her up to her feet.

'That sight . . . the boy's eyes were wide open, as they must have been when she fell on top of him. His nose, broken near the bridge, hardly protruded from his bluish face. No mouth: his lips, ground against his jaws by the immense pressure of her weight more effectively than by a hydraulic press, had been reduced to pulp – and yet traces of his beatific smile still lingered on his face. He wasn't breathing. Piggy, standing with her back to the galley cupboard, both hands covering her mouth, was staring at him with such enlarged eyes that for the first time I recognised the greenish colour of my Sea-Daughter's pupils. "Rose-Anne – move," I ordered. Trembling, mute apart from the faint wheezing of her shallow panting, she took a hesitant step back and let me through. Standing there, shaking from head to toe, in the middle of the galley, she obliterated all the space between the fridge on one side and the cupboards opposite. I opened the locker above the bench on which the Albanian was lying and rummaged for tissues. Amongst the stuff that fell out of it – safety harness, torch lamp, loo paper, plastic filters, all cascading down to Akzo's chest – was my old copy of Andersen's *Little Mermaid*, the one I had salvaged from *Hot Property*. I quickly emptied Akzo's mouth and wiped it as clean as I could. Then I knelt down next to him and, without bothering to check his pulse, started mouth-to-mouth resuscitation. I blew and blew and blew until I got dizzy. I kept at it long after my head started spinning and my eyesight blurred. I did not even have to block his squashed nose, since his nasal passages had been crushed. I breathed in deeply, blew into his mouth, waited for his chest to subside. And again. And again. And again. All the while I suspected I was wasting my time. He probably had died within five or ten minutes of Rose-Anne falling on him. This was a charade. Its real point was to delay the moment when I would have to turn around and face the woman who, for the last half hour, had vainly implored me to come and save her beloved husband. The woman whom I had failed for the second time. The woman whose salty tears were now silently falling over the nape of my neck as she bent forward, desperate for a spark of life on her lover's face. I hadn't heard her move, and wondered whether she was going to kill me. Nothing would have been easier. All she had to do was to let herself fall on top of me as I knelt, head twisted to the side, lips joined in a mortal kiss with the remnants of her lover's mouth.'

As Kurt stopped, lost in his harrowing memories, my mind wandered into reassuring legal territory. What would the legal position be in such a scenario? Would it be murder? How could the prosecution ever hope to prove it had been no accident?

Looking at Cathy in the faint pre-dawn glow, I noticed that her translucent pupils were so dilated that, in spite of her distraught, almost catatonic expression, she looked impossibly beautiful. It was time to conclude.

'Well – I take it Piggy did not kill you,' I said.

Kurt's eyes, now distinguishable in the pinkish light, remained blank.

'Alas – she showed no such mercy,' he murmured after a while. 'She put her hand on my shoulder, and, in a whisper so low I guessed the words more than heard them, ordered me out of the way. In the narrow confines of the galley, we swapped places again. She collapsed on the bench and carefully placed Akzo's head on her lap. Tears were streaming down her face, mixing with dried blood on her husband's lacerated lips, creating the impression that pinkish saliva was gurgling down his chin. She sat there for a long time, chanting the same words over and over: "Akzo – my love, my baby, what has he done to you? My darling, my poor love, what have I done to you? Akzo, my own love, my beloved husband, what shall I do without you?"

'Her fingers delicately ran over her lover's face; when they met the wide-open eyes, she drew both eyelids down, transforming his expression from one of childlike bewilderment to one of agitated sleep. She was oblivious of my presence and I remained speechless, acutely ashamed to be intruding on her grief, my heart crying for my little girl.

'"He was my life," she whispered eventually. She turned around and looked at me. "My whole life. All I had. All I ever shall have. A miracle. My angel. Why? Why did you have to destroy my life again? Wasn't once enough? How could you do it? What sort of a monster are you?"

'What was there to say?

'Several times she shook her head as though in disbelief, then turned back to Akzo and slowly started to clear all the rubbish that had accumulated on his body. She threw every item down on the floor until she got to the little book I had read her so often, the small children's book with, on its cover, the faded picture of a young and graceful mermaid with long fair hair, swimming at the crest of a foamy blue wave, surrounded by five extraordinarily red fish and two white seagulls; a shapely mermaid forlornly looking at the princely, wooden four-mast galleon that, far away, is sailing into an explosive orange dawn. With a strange smile, Rose-Anne picked up the book and absent-mindedly started turning the pages.

' "Are you my Sea-Dad?" she asked dreamily. "Tell me – what sort of a dad is that?"

'I moved forward and put my arms round her shoulders to stop her shaking.

' "Rose-Anne – yes, you used to be my Sea-Daughter. I'm sorry – so sorry – I've failed you. I failed you then – and now. But I always loved you. I have never hurt you intentionally – never. Please – you must at least believe that. I beg you."

' "Does it matter? Look at him. Just – look at him. My life . . . he was my whole life . . . never again . . ."

' "Everything your parents told you – all of that is false."

' "Does it matter?" she repeated. "Why should I care? Akzo is dead. Dead. Utterly dead. For ever dead. Don't you understand?"

'I remained silent.

' "Twice – you have killed me not once, but twice," she said without looking at me. "And each time you made a mess of it. What kind of a Sea-Dad are you? What do you think you deserve?"

'I bent over, picked up the Smith and Wesson that somehow had lodged itself between Akzo's legs, pressed it into her hand and kissed the tears on her lifeless eyes.

' "Rose-Anne, my lovely Sea-Daughter, do what you need to do," I whispered into her ear.

'Slowly, very slowly, she straightened up, turned around and pointed the gun at me. With her other hand she handed me the book. "Read the last page," she commanded.

'I obeyed, happy to die pleasing her – at last.

'I did not need to look at the page.

'She recited the words in perfect unison with me. It was one of those perfectly rehearsed duets in which both actors instinctively share breathing, rhythm, inflexion and tone. Amazingly, her voice had recovered the clear timbre and melodious purity that once belonged to my Sea-Daughter, and it felt as if we'd rehearsed together only the night before.

"The Little Mermaid looked at the sky. When the sun rose, she knew that she would die. She went into the tent where the Prince was asleep. She looked down at him, but she could not kill him. Instead, she took the knife and cast it far away in the waves. They shone red where it fell, as if drops of blood gurgled up from the water. Once again she gazed with aching eyes at the Prince. Then she threw herself into the sea, where she felt her body slowly dissolving into foam.

And now, the sun rose out of the sea."

'For one second we smiled at each other.

'She softly cursed me: "You deserve to live."

'Then she put the gun in her mouth and pulled the trigger.'

6

They say that tide and time change everything. Not for me. For me, everything changed in one single sticky night.

The quickening coolness of the small hours was no more. Only the shadow of the ill-assorted buildings on the hill to the east of the port protected us from the first beams of the sun. Nevertheless, in the light of a still-fresh morning, the port of Gruž, the city of Dubrovnik and the world were preparing themselves for a new day. A day when nothing would change and everything would be different.

I could now see that there were two types of bollard on the quay. The biggest ones, half a ton of elegant greenish bronze reminiscent of Napoleonic cannons, testified to past centuries of serious commercial activity. I felt almost embarrassed that the puny rope running from *Miss Lucy*'s port quarter should be made fast around such a monumental sculpture. Our starboard stern line, on the other hand, was secured around one of many miserly bitts which had recently sprouted when this quay had been allocated to yachting; a short steel cylinder filled with raw cement, already so rusty that the rare traces of blue paint were confined to its upper half. The contrast between past glory and present shabbiness was accentuated by the damage done to the paving stones underneath these new cleats, where the glistening patina left by millions of feet over perhaps half a millennium had made way to raw concrete. As the sun rose, these short bitts managed to cast long and spiky shadows.

I noticed we were sharing these bollards with several other vessels: Kurt's boat on one side; sailing yachts and a fast patrol boat, marked 'POLICIJA' in bold blue letters on her white hull, on the other. As the light kept improving, an impressive building became visible right ahead of us on the other side of the bay, golden with a red roof in front of a background of dark cypresses. It was on the waterfront, a peristyle of a dozen columns at its base, surmounted by a neo-classical entablature – incongruous but somehow pleasing.

There was a little town square close to us, where, alongside the busy road, dozens of people were setting up stalls and kiosks amongst higgledy-piggledy parked vans and pick-up trucks. We were too far away to distinguish the precise items being displayed, but a mixture of intuition, smells and colours suggested that a fresh fruit, vegetable and fish market would soon be in full swing. Very convenient, since most of our victuals would need replacing after the drenching of the previous day. To seaward, a greyish queue was building up on the ferries quay; already the old rust bucket moored there had started its generators, plumes of black diesel particulates escaping from its short funnel. On the waterfront, backpackers and locals were milling around the tired building which houses the offices of Jadrolinija, the ferry company, and the Café Barba, where business was brisk; just opposite, the tourist office wasn't open yet. Under the trees of the market square, two waiters were nonchalantly disposing tables and chairs on the small terrace of a whitewashed restaurant called Porat, which might well be worth checking out.

Cathy stretched her legs and sighed deeply. She seemed half asleep, but the tears at the corner of her eyes weren't yet dry. In the still-pale and indirect light, Kurt's face was so grey that even his eyes seemed discoloured.

'There you have it,' he said, staring vacantly at the classical temple across the water. 'Thank you for listening.'

I was dying to get up and stretch my legs.

'I'll go and check on Lucy,' I said.

But Cathy had already beaten me to it.

'No – I'll go!' she said. 'Christ – Terence, wasn't your watch supposed to ring every hour?'

She shot down the companionway. I remained on my feet, trying to get rid of the pins and needles in my legs.

'May I ask you a couple of questions?' I asked Kurt.

He gave no sign of having heard.

'Forgive me – but, as they say, once a lawyer, always a lawyer,' I continued. 'I was just wondering how you got your boat restarted. I mean, hadn't you thrown the engine keys into the sea?'

'Oh – that wasn't difficult,' he answered wearily. 'I had a spare set of keys at the bottom of a drawer. Even without those it would have taken me no more than fifteen minutes to wire the starter motors directly to the battery.'

'I understand. But then, if you started motoring at dawn yesterday, you should have been here around lunchtime, or perhaps in the early afternoon; what detained you until midnight?'

'You are absolutely right. But I spent the whole morning . . . drifting. I wasn't even trying to make plans; no, I was . . . stupefied. The mess . . . the sight of Rose-Anne, who again had fallen backwards on her husband's body . . . so heartbreaking that I ran to the saloon and just . . . collapsed. I guess I lay on the sofa for several hours, now prostrate, now in a kind of delirium. At some point I realised the life sentence passed on me by Rose-Anne would have to be served. If only because I owed Akzo and her a dignified burial. Since there was no question of my being able to bury them at sea all by myself, I had to bring them ashore.'

'Why Dubrovnik? You must have been much closer to Albania?'

'Albania?' He sounded incredulous. 'Too risky, too much of an unknown. On the other hand, not only do I know the port of Dubrovnik well, but the German consul here is a friend. So, yesterday afternoon, I gathered my strength and dragged each and every one of Akzo's heavy crates overboard. Then I restarted the engines and headed north towards Croatia, catching a glimpse of the electric storm that mauled you on the way. That's why I only got here a few hours ago, in the middle of the night.'

I nodded silently, uncomfortably aware of the macabre cargo lying a few feet away inside the motorboat, separated from us by no more than half an inch of glass-reinforced plastic. At least the morning breeze was taking the stench away from us.

'What do you think is going to happen to me?' he asked.

'Well, as long as your story is corroborated by evidence on the boat, you should be all right,' I replied. 'Of course you'll get a tremendous amount of hassle from the authorities – turning up with a cargo of dead bodies tends to have that effect on most officials. If you wish, I can make sure that you get proper legal representation.'

'That would be most kind. Thank you. I'll need it.'

'I'd better go down and see how Cathy is getting on,' I said.

'May I come with you?'

'Of course. You must at least have a cup of coffee before you go.'

Before I'd got to the bottom of the companionway steps, I knew something was wrong. The silence . . . It was the silence. I could hear neither Lucy nor Cathy. I rushed to the forecabin and stopped at the door. Cathy was crumpled on the floor, elbows around her knees, her shoulders shaken by an almost unbroken series of silent, convulsive sobs. With the uncomprehending eyes of a terrified animal, she looked up at me – then shrivelled again in a distraught heap. Lucy, my Lucy, pale as death under her sickening vine-dark nightcap, was lying rigid, straight in the middle of the bunk, a frown on her sweet little face and her eyes shut, arms neatly extended, palms up, on either side of her trunk. Her well-adjusted Mermaid pyjamas modestly revealed no more than her delicate waxen feet. My eyes went from her to Cathy and back, unable to make sense of the scene.

'Lucy!' I called. 'Lucy! Wake up, baby!'

She did not stir. Cathy's spasmodic sobbing, silent though it was, now deafened me. I took a step forward, bent down and slowly moved my hand towards Lucy, concerned not to frighten her, but determined to wake her up gently.

'Out!' Kurt growled behind me. I turned around in utter confusion. 'Out of my way!' he repeated.

Bemused, I took a step back and let him through.

'Cathy – please go,' he ordered.

She ignored him.

'Now!' he snarled.

She did not react.

He bent over, grabbed her by the arm with his one good hand and, before I could protest or resist, threw us back a couple of feet. By then we were out of the cabin. In a flash he locked the door behind us. As though paralysed, Cathy lay at my feet. I dropped down to the floor and put my right arm over her shuddering shoulders.

'Kurt – for God's sake – what the hell do you think you're doing, man?' I shouted. 'Are you out of your bloody mind? Open the door immediately!'

For the next few minutes I had the distinct feeling that I, the only sane person left on *Miss Lucy*, was fast going mad. Sleep deprivation and physical exhaustion conspired to deprive me of my grip on reality. Why was my wife crying on the floor? Lucy? Rose-Anne? Which boat were we on? What could a stranger be doing on this boat, locked up with my sweet baby? I could hear his low voice droning on through the cabin door. Was he telling Lucy a story? What kind of a resuscitation technique was that? My attempts to hold on to lucidity only caused regrets and recriminations to start welling up inside my head. Lucy should have received proper medical care. My fault. I had talked Cathy out of this sensible course of action. *Because I was afraid of what a delirious Lucy might say, I had failed to alert Cathy to her worsening condition.* It was my fault. My fault entirely.

I had to break down the cabin door. My hand was already on its handle when it suddenly opened.

Kurt stood in the doorway.

On his left arm, he was carrying Lucy.

The first thing I noticed was: she was naked. Her arms were round his powerful neck.

I felt I was inexorably losing it. Losing the plot. What the hell . . .

'The Mer-King . . .' Lucy whispered with a happy, tired little smile.

Kurt knelt down next to Cathy and carefully transferred Lucy into her arms. I was reminded of the midwife who, six years ago, in a similar gesture, had entrusted Cathy with the same tiny, bloodied body.

'You must go to hospital – now,' he commanded, offering her his good hand. 'Every minute counts.'

For a moment, Cathy did not react. She just sat on the floor, looking at her daughter. Then at Kurt. At Lucy. Then at me. Incredulous. Dumbstruck. After a while she grabbed Kurt's hand, pulled herself up, picked up a dirty multicolour bathing towel, wrapped Lucy in it and said: 'Right. Move. Now.'

I grabbed my mobile telephone and the pouch containing our wet passports, my wallet and the ship's documents. Already on the first step of the companionway, Cathy turned back towards Kurt and whispered: 'Werther – what about you?'

'I'd better wait for the authorities on board my boat. Then I'll follow you to hospital – hopefully. We'll meet again. Lucy will be all right.'

'Werther – thank you. Thank you for Lucy. I'll never forget you. Thank you thank you thank you. Your story . . . I hope you know your story is in good hands.'

'That I know,' he replied. 'Forgive me – I could not take the risk of letting lies and falsehoods become the official truth. Not for a second time. I hope your husband understands this.'

'I understand,' Cathy said. 'Katharina is a lucky woman. She's never been lied to. Nor will she ever be lied to. Not by you, anyway.'

She took a quick step down and stood in front of Kurt for a second. Without smiling, he looked her in the eyes and put his left hand on Lucy's head. Cathy raised herself on her tiptoes and kissed him quickly. Then she turned to me and said: 'I am on my way, Terence.'

I followed her up the five steps of the companionway, Kurt hard on my heels. As we reached the cockpit we saw two uniformed men standing on the quay. Although both sported oversized caps and pistols, one was wearing a khaki uniform, while the other was clad in navy blue.

'Thank you, captain,' I said to Kurt as Cathy, carrying our treasure, carefully started walking down the gangplank. 'What are you actually going to do?'

'My story has been told. I found my Sea-Daughter; I have been reunited with Katharina. Much more to the point: what are *you* going to do, Herr Garfield?'

I looked into his blue eyes. They were inscrutable.

'Some people go to sea to escape the truth,' he continued. 'But you cannot. The sea never lies. The sea does not tolerate lies. If you do not come clean, the sea, the rotting sea punishes you: it washes you on to some terrifying, alien shore. And leaves you there to rot. Perhaps you forgot that?'

I was at a loss for words, unable to sustain his stare. With stooped shoulders, he turned around and slowly walked up the side deck towards the bows, looking for the easiest way to leave *Miss Lucy* and clamber back on to his own boat. As he reached the guardrail, he stopped, took something out of his pocket and, holding it in his clenched fist, raised his left arm towards the rising sun in a kind of salute. Then, arm fully extended in a ceremonial gesture, he slowly opened his fingers and let their contents fall into the water. It was Lucy's pyjamas. Lucy's

Mermaid pyjamas. Both top and bottom remained afloat, one foot apart, bobbing up and down amid the foam and scum.

'She's a mermaid no more. Leave her be!' he shouted.

A few seconds later Kurt – or was it Werther? – had disappeared inside his floating mortuary.

'Terence! Are you coming?' Cathy called from ashore.

She had somehow talked the young man in the navy-blue uniform into providing us with emergency transport; indeed, he was opening for her the door of an official-looking Renault with a strobe light on its roof. As the car started, the man in green, possibly some kind of customs officer, was making his way up *Gwelan II*'s gangplank.

I lowered myself into the rear seat next to Cathy and shut the door. The driver immediately made a racing start.

'I wonder how the hospital will be,' Cathy said.

'I'm sure it'll be all right,' I answered. 'Hopefully they'll let you stay with Lucy. That's the main thing.'

'My God!' she sighed. 'What a night . . . and how unlucky that man has been! Makes one think, doesn't it?'

'Do you believe his story?' I asked.

'Of course! Why should he lie to us?'

'Well . . . by his own admission he has two bodies on his boat. That was always going to take some explaining.'

'Nonsense,' she said. 'Believe me: that man was speaking the truth. By the way, what was he saying when he left? You know, about Lucy not being a mermaid any more, and you having to leave her alone?'

'Is that what he said? I have no idea.'

Something made her look at me and tighten her grasp on Lucy, who was dozing on her lap.

'You heard what he said. I was already on the quay – and I heard it clearly.'

She was fixing me with a frown, deep in thought. I looked away.

'Terence,' Cathy said.

'Uh?'

'Terence, look at me. Look at me! I know about Sarah. And it hurts . . . obviously more than you can ever imagine. But I can forgive you for that. For Lucy's sake.'

'Sarah? What Sarah? What on earth are you talking about? Are you crazy? What's Sarah got to do with Kurt – or with anything?'

'But,' she continued steadfastly, 'if you have messed up with Lucy – that's something else. God forbid, Terence – if you have but lifted a finger – ever – even once – I shall never forgive you. Never.'

With screeching tyres, the driver took a right turn so fast that Cathy slid into me. I put my shaking hand on her knee.

'Cathy, for God's sake . . .' I protested as we skidded to a halt in front of the hospital.

But she had already stormed out of the car.

Our driver had a quick word with a nurse who took a close look at Lucy. Then, pointing me towards a tired armchair, the nurse invited Cathy to follow her. I stood watching as Cathy, still carrying Lucy, unsteadily walked to the end of the long corridor and disappeared without looking back; then I collapsed into the low, stained armchair and found myself alone.

Christ   this was a bloody near miss   how long has Cathy known about Sarah   unbelievable   why the hell didn't she say anything   fucking unbelievable   perhaps she was only bluffing and I fell for it   unlikely though   she bloody knows   I wonder how she found out   maybe Sarah spilled the beans in a fit of pique   more than once she has teased me about doing exactly that   I have always studiously ignored these jokes   who the fuck cares   it doesn't matter a damn now   at least we made it to hospital   let's hope these guys know what they are doing   it feels good being a family all three of us together   that's all I want   I want to see Lucy grow up   I want my life to continue   God I am so relieved that my affair with Sarah is over   it nearly fucked up my whole life   it really did   I just want to grow old with Cathy simple easy no complications   I won't even object if she calls me Terry   she can call me anything she bloody well likes   how fucking stupid can a man be   this whole affair was daft pointless unnecessary   but Cathy and I love each other   it will work out   has to work out   we'll be all right   Lucy will be all right   am I still awake or dreaming   being the only one awake on watch as it were there is a good feeling   a perfect husband and a reformed father   that's going to be me   that *is* me   Kurt is right   I must leave Lucy alone   no messing about   everyone is entitled to a second chance   Cathy will soon forget about this madman   what does he know anyway   I'll see them all right   will Lucy be all right   nothing is less certain   she looks pathetic poor angel   all that dried blood on her head   awful   God   I had such an unbelievable undeservedly fortunate life   a life that without my wife or daughter would be no more   I just want it to continue   is that asking too much   my elbow hurts like white-hot hell   shit I'm feeling sick   what's the point of hospitals if nobody ever looks after you   true I have done no more to deserve happiness than Kurt to be damned   the poor bastard certainly did not get a second chance   hardly got a chance at all really   who cares who the fuck cares   OK I might well owe happiness to blind chance more than merit   so what am I supposed to do   turn my back on it   BEEP-BEEP BEEP-BEEP   my stupid phone is beeping like mad   of course it's been off for several days   no point in going sailing if people can still harass you   dozens of voice and text messages   memory full   I'll need to call the office   organise repatriation   BEEP-BEEP BEEP-BEEP OK OK!   just one second

Menu.
Messages.
Select.
Scroll down.
Inbox.
Select.
'Sarah Mobile'.
Select.

TERENCE CALL URGENTLY RE OPERATION ORE. POLICE HAVE SEIZED YR OFFICE COMPUTER AND BROKEN INTO YR HOME. WANT 2 INTERVIEW YOU URGENTLY. SARAH

WHAT? . . . I am reading this again and again and again and again   cannot believe it   my exhausted brain just *cannot* make sense of it – Operation Ore – for Christ's sake I'm a *lawyer* not a criminal   what do the cops think they're doing taking my office and home computers away   so they have found the pictures of my little mermaid   the pictures I used to post on the Internet   - she's so beautiful   what's wrong with sharing her?

Do you think I'd ever harm her – my beautiful Lucy?

Why are you not answering?

Have you been listening?

Please don't go yet – wait a moment – I am so lonely in my cage.

A NOTE ON THE AUTHOR

Yves Bonavero was born and educated in Paris. He worked in the City of London for fourteen years until at the age of thirty-seven he founded Bonaparte Films. In 1999 he graduated from Oxford University with a First in philosophy and German. *Something In the Sea* is his first novel. He lives in London.

A NOTE ON THE TYPE

The text of this book is set in Linotype Sabon, named after the type founder, Jacques Sabon. It was designed by Jan Tschichold and jointly developed by Linotype, Monotype and Stempel, in response to a need for a typeface to be available in identical form for mechanical hot metal composition and hand composition using foundry type.

Tschichold based his design for Sabon roman on a font engraved by Garamond, and Sabon italic on a font by Granjon. It was first used in 1966 and has proved an enduring modern classic.